JAMES BERRY was born and grew up in Jamaica, and now lives both there and in Sussex. He is a distinguished writer and poet. In 1982 he won the National Poetry Society's Annual Prize for *Fantasy of an African Boy*, and in 1987 *A Thief in the Village* was the Grand Prix winner of the Smarties Prize.

Books by James Berry

JAMES BERRY

A THIEF IN THE VILLAGE

AND OTHER STORIES

A PUFFIN BOOK

PUFFIN BOOKS

UK | USA | Canada | Ireland | Australia
India | New Zealand | South Africa

Puffin Books is part of the Penguin Random House group of companies
whose addresses can be found at global.penguinrandomhouse.com.

www.penguin.co.uk
www.puffin.co.uk
www.ladybird.co.uk

First published by Hamish Hamilton Children's Books 1987
Published in Puffin Books 1989
Reissued in this edition 2016
002

Copyright © James Berry, 1987
All rights reserved

Set in 12.5/16.5 pt Sabon LT Std
Typeset by Jouve (UK), Milton Keynes
Printed and bound in Great Britain by Clays Ltd, Elcograf S.p.A.

A CIP catalogue record for this book is available from the British Library

ISBN: 978-0-141-36864-1

All correspondence to:
Puffin Books
Penguin Random House Children's
80 Strand, London WC2R 0RL

MIX
Paper from
responsible sources
FSC   FSC® C018179
www.fsc.org

Penguin Random House is committed to a
sustainable future for our business, our readers
and our planet. This book is made from Forest
Stewardship Council® certified paper.

Contents

Contents

1. Becky and the Wheels-and-brake Boys

EVEN my own cousin Ben was there – riding away, in the ringing of bicycle bells down the road. Every time I came to watch them – see them riding round and round enjoying themselves – they scooted off like crazy on their bikes.

They can't keep doing that. They'll see!

I only want to be with Nat, Aldo, Jimmy and Ben. It's no fair reason they don't want to be with me. Anybody could go off their head for that. Anybody! A girl can not, not, let boys get away with it all the time.

Bother! I have to walk back home, alone.

I know total-total that if I had my own bike, the Wheels-and-brake Boys wouldn't treat me like that. I'd just ride away with them, wouldn't I?

Over and over I told my mum I wanted a bike. Over and over she looked at me as if I was crazy. 'Becky, d'you think you're a boy? Eh? D'you think you're a boy? In any case, where's the money to come from? Eh?'

Of course I know I'm not a boy. Of course I know I'm not crazy. Of course I know all that's no reason why I can't have a bike. No reason! As soon as I get indoors I'll just have to ask again – ask Mum once more.

At home, indoors, I didn't ask my mum.

It was evening time, but sunshine was still big patches in yards and on housetops. My two younger brothers, Lenny and Vin, played marbles in the road. Mum was taking measurements of a boy I knew, for his new trousers and shirt. Mum made clothes for people. Meggie, my sister two years younger than me, was helping Mum on the verandah. Nobody would be pleased with me not helping. I began to help.

Granny-Liz would always stop fanning herself to drink up a glass of iced water. I gave my granny a glass of iced water, there in her rocking-chair. I looked in the kitchen to find shelled coconut pieces to cut into small cubes for the fowls' morning feed. But Granny-Liz had done it. I came and started tidying up bits and pieces of cut-off material around my mum on the floor. My sister got nasty, saying she was already helping Mum. Not a single good thing was happening for me.

With me even being all so thoughtful of Granny's need of a cool drink, she started up some botheration against me.

Listen to Granny-Liz: 'Becky, with you moving about me here on the verandah, I hope you don't have any centipedes or scorpions in a jam jar in your pocket.'

'No, mam,' I said sighing, trying to be calm. 'Granny-Liz,' I went on, 'you forgot. My centipede and scorpion died.' All the same, storm broke against me.

'Becky,' my mum said. 'You know I don't like you wandering off after dinner. Haven't I told you I don't want you keeping company with those awful riding-about bicycle boys? Eh?'

'Yes, mam.'

'Those boys are a menace. Riding bicycles on sidewalks and narrow paths together, ringing bicycle bells and braking at people's feet like wild bulls charging anybody, they're heading for trouble.'

'They're the Wheels-and-brake Boys, mam.'

'The what?'

'The Wheels-and-brake Boys.'

'Oh! Given themselves a name as well, have they? Well, Becky, answer this. How d'you always manage to look like you've just escaped from a hair-pulling battle? Eh? And don't I tell you not to break the back down and wear your canvas shoes like slippers? Don't you ever hear what I say?'

'Yes, mam.'

'D'you want to end up a field labourer? Like where your father used to be overseer?'

'No, mam.'

'Well, Becky, will you please go off and do your homework?'

Everybody did everything to stop me. I was allowed no chance whatsoever. No chance to talk to Mum about the bike I dream of day and night! And I knew exactly the bike I wanted. I wanted a bike like Ben's bike. Oh, I wished I still had even my scorpion on a string to run up and down somebody's back!

I answered my mum. 'Yes, mam.' I went off into Meg's and my bedroom.

I sat down at the little table, as well I might. Could homework stay in anybody's head in broad daylight outside? No. Could I keep a bike like Ben's out of my head? Not one bit. That bike took me all over the place. My beautiful bike jumped every log, every rock, every fence. My beautiful bike did everything cleverer than a clever cowboy's horse, with me in the saddle. And the bell, the bell was such a glorious gong of a ring!

If Dad was alive I could talk to him. If Dad was alive he'd give me money for the bike like a shot.

I sighed. It was amazing what a sigh could do. I sighed and tumbled on a great idea. Tomorrow evening I'd get Shirnette to come with me. Both of us together would be sure to get the boys interested to teach us to ride. Wow! With Shirnette they can't just ride away!

Next day at school everything went sour. For the first time, Shirnette and me had a real fight, because of what I hated most.

Shirnette brought a cockroach to school in a shoe-polish tin. At playtime she opened the tin and let the cockroach fly into my blouse. Pure panic and disgust nearly killed me. I crushed up the cockroach in my clothes and practically ripped my blouse off, there in open sunlight. Oh the smell of a cockroach is the nastiest ever to block your nose! I started running with my blouse to go and wash it. Twice I had to stop and be sick.

I washed away the crushed cockroach stain from my blouse. Then the stupid Shirnette had to come into the toilet, falling about laughing. All right, I knew the cockroach treatment was for the time when I made my centipede on a string crawl up Shirnette's back. But you put fair-is-fair aside. I just barged into Shirnette.

When it was all over I had on a wet blouse, but Shirnette had one on too.

Then going home with the noisy flock of children from school I had ever such a new, new idea. If Mum thought I was scruffy, Nat, Aldo, Jimmy and Ben might think so too. I didn't like that.

After dinner, I combed my hair in the bedroom. Mum did her machining on the verandah. Meggie helped Mum. Granny sat there, wishing she could take on any job, as usual.

I told Mum I was going to make up a quarrel with Shirnette. I went, but my friend wouldn't speak to me, let alone come out to keep my company. I stood alone and watched the Wheels-and-brake Boys again.

This time the boys didn't race away past me. I stood leaning against the tall coconut palm tree. People passed up and down. The nearby main road was busy with traffic. But I didn't mind. I watched the boys. Riding round and round the big Flame-tree, Nat, Aldo, Jimmy and Ben looked marvellous.

At first each boy rode round the tree alone. Then each boy raced each other round the tree, going round three times. As he won, the winner rang his bell on and on, till he stopped panting and could laugh and talk properly. Next, most reckless and fierce, all the boys raced against each other. And, leaning against their bicycles, talking and joking, the boys popped soft drinks open, drank and ate chipped bananas.

I walked up to Nat, Aldo, Jimmy and Ben and said, 'Can somebody teach me to ride?'

'Why don't you stay indoors and learn to cook and sew and wash clothes?' Jimmy said.

I grinned. 'I know all that already,' I said. 'And one day perhaps I'll even be mum to a boy child, like all of you. Can you cook and sew and wash clothes, Jimmy? All I want is to learn to ride. I want you to teach me.'

I didn't know why I said what I said. But everybody went silent and serious.

One after the other, Nat, Aldo, Jimmy and Ben got on to their bikes and rode off. I wasn't at all cross with them. I only wanted to be riding out of the playground with them. I knew they'd be heading into the town to have ice-cream and things and talk and laugh.

Mum was sitting alone on the verandah. She sewed buttons on to a white shirt she'd made. I sat down next to Mum. Straightaway, 'Mum,' I said, 'I still want to have a bike badly.'

'Oh, Becky, you still have that foolishness in your head? What am I going to do?'

Mum talked with some sympathy. Mum knew I was honest. 'I can't get rid of it, mam,' I said.

Mum stopped sewing. 'Becky,' she said, staring in my face, 'how many girls around here do you see with bicycles?'

'Janice Gordon has a bike,' I reminded her.

'Janice Gordon's dad has acres and acres of coconuts and bananas, with a business in the town as well.'

I knew Mum was just about to give in. Then my granny had to come out on to the verandah and interfere. Listen to that Granny-Liz. 'Becky, I heard your mother tell you over and over she can't afford to buy you a bike. Yet you keep on and on. Child, you're a girl.'

'But I don't want a bike because I'm a girl.'

'D'you want it because you feel like a boy?' Granny said.

'No. I only want a bike because I want it and want it and want it.'

Granny just carried on. 'A tomboy's like a whistling woman and a crowing hen, who can only come to a bad end. D'you understand?'

I didn't want to understand. I knew Granny's speech was an awful speech. I went and sat down with Lenny and Vin, who were making a kite.

By Saturday morning I felt real sorry for Mum. I could see Mum really had it hard for money. I had to try and help. I knew anything of Dad's – anything – would be worth a great mighty hundred pounds.

I found myself in the centre of town, going through the busy Saturday crowd. I hoped Mum wouldn't be too cross. I went into the fire station. With lots of luck I came face to face with a round face man in uniform. He talked to me. 'Little miss, can I help you?'

I told him I'd like to talk to the head man. He took me into the office and gave me a chair. I sat down. I opened out my brown paper parcel. I showed him my dad's sun helmet. I told him I thought it would make a good fireman's hat. I wanted to sell the helmet for some money towards a bike, I told him.

The fireman laughed a lot. I began to laugh too. The fireman put me in a car and drove me back home.

Mum's eyes popped to see me bringing home the fireman. The round face fireman laughed at my adventure. Mum laughed too, which was really good. The fireman gave Mum my dad's hat back. Then, mystery, mystery, Mum sent me outside while they talked.

My mum was only a little cross with me. Then – mystery and more mystery – my mum took me with the fireman in his car to his house.

The fireman brought out what? A bicycle! A beautiful, shining bicycle! His nephew's bike. His nephew had been taken away, all the way to America. The bike had been left with the fireman-uncle for him to sell it. And the good kind fireman-uncle decided we could have the bike – on small payments. My mum looked uncertain. But, in a big, big way the fireman knew it was all right. And Mum smiled a little. My mum had good sense to know it was all right. My mum took the bike from the fireman Mister Dean.

And guess what? Seeing my bike much, much newer than his, my cousin Ben's eyes popped with envy. But – he took on the big job. He taught me to ride. Then he taught Shirnette.

I ride into town with the Wheels-and-brake Boys now. When she can borrow a bike, Shirnette comes too. We all sit together. We have patties and ice-cream and drink drinks together. We talk and joke. We ride about, all over the place.

And, again, guess what? Fireman Mister Dean became our best friend, and Mum's especially. He started coming round almost every day.

2. A Thief in the Village

I'D COME back to school with the story. My father had told me the story. He'd gone deep into it. He himself and my aunt were featured as two main characters in the story, when they were teenagers. My father had pointed out other people who were there as characters in the story too.

My parents came from Jamaica. But because I was born in London, and live and go to school there, I never dreamt I could've become so fascinated by my father's birthplace and home village.

True, three summers I spent in the village were fantastic. I had glorious sunshine and sea and swimming and boating. I helped with different animals in backyards. Trees with huge leaves and different fruits made me wonder, made me happy enjoying them. And like the women, men, boys and girls, I rode a donkey or a mule up to fields in wooded and open hills, where we cooked meals on an open fire.

I was a visitor yet I was a part of everybody. The people treated me like their long lost village princess. And they had no doubts about how their village language and voices thrilled me something big. Each time, my holiday was just brilliant with all sorts of fresh fun. Of a truth, from somewhere halfway through the first holiday I started to feel as if I'd always lived in the village.

My English teacher Mr Wills bumped into my gang of friends listening to me telling my dad's story. Mr Wills stopped. He joined the gang. And though I saw him there listening he didn't put me off one bit. I just sailed on performing in my style of Jamaican village voices. True, English was my best subject. All this time, in my year, I seemed to pop up tops with English. And Mr Wills always gave me loads of his interest in my work. He told me what to do; he pushed me on like any athletics trainer.

Yet at the end of the story when Mr Wills said, 'Maxine, I'd like you to write down all of that story,' I panicked.

'What, sir? You got to be joking,' I said, really worried.

'No joke,' he said. 'I would like you to write it down. All of it.'

I had to go away to think about it. I came back to Mr Wills. I asked him if, in the story, I could call my father and auntie by their home 'pet names'.

'Yes. Certainly.' he said. 'Exactly as they were called then at home, as teenagers.'

I was anxious; I was excited. Yet the story flowed easily on to paper, as I'd heard it, and told it . . .

Something flew swiftly across the side of their faces. Nenna threw her head back and said, 'Wha' was that?'

Her brother Man-Man didn't stir a muscle. His finger against the trigger of the double-barrelled shotgun just stayed there. The gun was held down at his side, all firm and solid. His answer clipped Nenna something scornful. 'Don't you know a ratbat?'

She stayed silent. Not a word from Nenna now. The coconut plantation was one shadow of night. But looking up between the long and vague palm leaves, they had the distant stars twinkling their presence with them. They'd been here some time now. Yet they still felt trapped in a big cage of noisy night creatures and quiet creepy-crawlies. Ratbats in scores flew and crisscrossed and charged about like crazy things in darkness. They flapped about with each other and squeaked in branches. Juicy ripe mangoes the bats dipped in and fought over were strong with sweet smell on warm air. The place was alive. Owls hooted, hidden in darkness. Insects chirped. But then wasn't night like day to all this winged life? Wasn't man the interloper, who should be in bed? Well, Man-Man and Nenna were no interlopers. They'd come to catch interlopers, man or woman, who'd come to steal coconuts.

It didn't bother the brother and sister. They were out in the open night doing their father's job. At four o'clock that morning their parents had mounted their two-mule cart, loaded with yams, watermelons, plantains, coconut-oil, chickens, eggs, pimento berries, nutmegs, firewood, off to market in the city, Kingston. Man-Man and Nenna took it their duty to be exposed in the plantation, as swallowed figures in darkness, between towered-up coconut palm trees. Back to back, they stood against one of the smooth-trunked coconut trees. Man-Man wore his father's motor-tyre sandals. Nenna wore Man-Man's village-made boots, with the iron horse-shoes on the heels. Nenna was as tall as Man-Man. But she wouldn't question it that he held on to the gun.

Nenna was the only village schoolgirl to go 'walking property', and with a gun, though it was her first time. And after it, both girls and boys at school never stopped asking her questions about it. They made it look as if she'd been overseas or to the moon or something.

So all this waiting-for-a-thief was new to Nenna. Man-Man had patrolled many a dark field with their father. Now he was showing Nenna how to keep ears, keep eyes, pointed; penetrating deep night, listening, looking, for sound or movement, well knowing an interloper could see them before they saw him. And sometimes they thought they heard low voices. Sometimes they thought they saw movements. Other times they were sure they heard the heavy dropping thuds of picked coconuts falling. True, most of these happenings came from Nenna's vivid imagination. True, her brother knew she was excited, yet ignored none of her fanciful reports.

'Where did you hear that?' he would say.

'Comin' from where the owl is hootin', she answered.

'Where did you hear that this time?'

'Over by those short coconut trees toward the hillside there.'

'Now where did you hear that?'

'Over there.'

'Over there where?'

She pointed. 'In the darknis there, toward the corner of the distric', where houses stop.'

Each time she thought she heard a sound they stopped their breath; they watched; they listened; they ignored time and stars and bats and insects. And not once did her false alarm spark off her big brother into anything mouthy. It was terrific how they were great comrades.

Then he began to talk slowly in his quiet and ominous voice. 'So the fellow Big-Walk still didn' say anyt'ing at all, eh?'

Straightaway she knew what he meant. 'No,' she said. 'Not a word to anybody. But, he well know he cornered. I t'ink he well aware of that.'

'You t'ink so?'

'Yes, man.'

'Why? He did look frighten?'

'Well, he did jus' look like he know he cornered.'

Everyone knew Big-Walk sold coconuts that couldn't have come off his land. People's fields got plundered and pilched right and left. Pigs, goats, fowls went missing. Everybody knew these things got ended up in Big-Walk's lonely kitchen or deep in the woods for one-man feasts. But the man was like a slippery eel in a river. And Man-Man didn't stop talking about him readily.

'You t'ink we goin' get we hands on Mas' Big-Walk tonight?'

'Well –' Nenna stopped. It suddenly seemed to her that perhaps everybody was accusing Big-Walk just because he was so different. But then, she thought, evidence was really against the man, lots of it.

' "Well" what?' her brother pressed. 'Don't you believe the man mus' one day walk before police, with proof? Don't you t'ink he mus' get caught?'

She agreed with her brother. They started to get excited. Remembering not to give themselves away to any lurking interloper, they began to whisper. Their low voices were still excited. They talked about that meeting with Big-Walk two evenings before.

Practically everybody had wanted to hear about that meeting. She'd gone over it again tonight, while they'd waited on their thatched roof verandah before field-watch. Except for the baby asleep, their younger brothers and sisters had stayed up with them to wait on the moon to go down. And while the moon kept its eye on them, through the tangle of creeping honeysuckle on one side of their verandah, they discussed Big-Walk endlessly.

Nenna's meeting with Big-Walk had really happened because her father always took a bottle of cheap white rum whenever he made the seventy-mile journey to market in the city.

Events had really moved nippily. Up at the village square getting the rum, first of all, she'd seen a number of men keeping company in the rum bar. Leaning and sitting and drinking together, they were the District Constable, Mister Anderson; Duke, the town-man who lodged with the schoolmaster; Uncle Slim, a man who laughed most of the time; Cousin Dago, the man who always bragged how the biggest yams came out of his field.

The men's faces had been moist with sweat from the heat, their rum-drinking, and their excited, non-stop talking. The D.C. remembered he wanted to sell his donkey. In a brief silence he said, 'Duke, I tellin' you I sellin' mi jackass Victor. I want buy a mule who wi' bring down mo' bananas from mountain lan'.'

Duke had answered in a happy, friendly way. 'D.C. you know I deal in field produce, not donkeys. You know that, man.'

The men had been in a friendly, merry mood. Before the D.C. could answer, everybody'd burst out saying something all at the same time and instantly stopped, with a hush. They'd heard the shopkeeper call the name 'Big-Walk'. The men had looked at one another, tossed their drinks down quickly and followed Nenna through the swinging halfdoors. They'd all come into the main part of the all-purpose country shop.

The tall, ragged man with knotted beard and matted-looking hair was there. His black mongrel sat alertly at his feet. The bottom of the man's trousers had frayed away to his shin, way above his broad bare feet with their spreading toes. His piece of old shirt, more skimpy than a waistcoat, was held together with a knot at his naked navel. His sheathed dagger was hung from his belt and his dirty hessian bag slung round his shoulder. He wore a broad leather strap round his wrist. And, as always, he held his sword-sharp machete in his hand. He was really a tall and marvellously muscular man. He'd come to do his shopping.

The name Big-Walk popped up visions of holes left in yam hills and the yams gone; and a missing pig, a missing goat; and fowls squawking and fluttering at their roost at night in the midst of quick, escaping footsteps. The name meant a man who'd disappear from his hut for weeks and then suddenly come back; a man who'd walk through the village and never say a word, never a how-de-do, to woman, man or child. He gave nothing and got nothing. And since his return from prison, thieving had hotted up. Yet Big-Walk's prison sentence hadn't come about on a stealing charge.

He'd been arrested on suspicion of stealing and butchering a hog, and running away leaving behind a hessian bag. But he'd been released on lack of real evidence. Another time, arrested with equal confidence for stealing a ram goat, he'd been quickly released. Another time, after a fierce outcry from three villagers, who'd suffered losses the same night, the D.C. had collected a party of men. Around midday the men had arrived at Big-Walk's place up in the bush.

Keeping their distance, the police party had spied on Big-Walk through tangled growths of leaves and vines. They'd seen him chopping wood, seen him swimming with his dog up and down the river that ran through his land. He'd settled in his hammock with his dog when the police had pounced on him and searched his hut. They'd found nothing to pin on Big-Walk. Disappointed, they'd decided to make a thorough search of his two-acre piece of land. It was then that the police had tumbled on his small patch of marijuana growing. 'It only I who smoke it,' Big-Walk had pleaded. And he'd been imprisoned for growing the illegal 'weed'.

A small crowd of people had gathered in the shop from nowhere. Youths leaned against the shop in fits to hold back laughter; children were whispering and tittering; their mothers jeered at 'some people who get fat on other people's things'. In all this, Big-Walk made sure nobody came too close to him. Frequently he swung his head round in a full half circle, flashing wide suspicious eyes.

But before he'd collected up his sugar, flour, matches and paraffin oil, the men standing around him had started hollering.

'You see that!' Cousin Dago drummed up deeply. 'You see, he don't buy meat. He don't buy fish. Yet look 'pon the size of the man neck. Look 'pon big shoulder an' big muscle them. Look how the man look like he a race horse.'

'An' look 'pon the man dog,' Uncle Slim followed up in high-pitched voice. And somehow he alone laughed.

But Cousin Dago took up his point. 'Yes, man. Look how the black dog roun' an' shiny.'

'Dago,' Uncle Slim went on, 'how about you an' me givin' weself a invite to one a them one-man feast what go on up the bush?'

'You know, Slim, we might even taste a piece of we own chicken,' Cousin Dago said. And the whole shop laughed together, except the serious and wild-looking man.

And Big-Walk had pushed his grocery into his hessian bag and started paying the shopkeeper.

Cousin Dago roared, 'Big-Walk, you forgettin' meat, you forgettin' fish!'

With perfect timing, the people picked up the words and chanted, 'Big-Walk, you forgettin' meat, you forgettin' fish! Big-Walk, you forgettin' meat, you forgettin' fish!'

The big, ragged man had only adjusted the weight of his bag on his shoulder and walked out of the shop with his dog. The people gave him a shower of insults and abuses to see him off. But Big-Walk had not looked back. A lady last of all said, 'Never mind Mister Big-Walk: "Bucket going to the well every day one day it bottom will drop out."'

Nenna had wondered over the lady's country proverb. So often somebody said something like that which came true. She'd wondered if she and Man-Man would really get Big-Walk shackled up.

Anger turned into jokes. But some bitterness still hung around the shop after Big-Walk had left. It had taken Duke to sweeten up the atmosphere by handing out free cigarettes.

Then, smoking one of them, the District Constable said, 'What a disgrace havin' a man like that in you' own distric'!'

Duke said, 'Mister Anderson, you are the law in this distric'.'

'Listen,' the D.C. said, changing the subject.

'I'm all ears.'

'You know somet'n', man?'

'What?'

'You could tek my jackass in you' van an' sell it. At top price. Considerin' a commission fo' you'self.'

Duke thought about the D.C.'s suggestion and said he'd prefer to go out and find a buyer first. The two men shook hands warmly on the deal, with Duke grinning, showing his gold tooth.

It wasn't surprising that the D.C. liked the town man. Duke knew about what was happening in the city and what went on in the world. Duke and the D.C. drank and talked and laughed together more than with anybody else. In fact most people liked Duke. From here he took in other villages around, buying the food and vegetables and fruit he took back to town to sell. He'd become a special city link for the village. People asked him to buy and bring back things from the city for them. When his red van pulled up in the square, mothers, fathers and children always flocked round it. And always he called out, 'Hi, country friends!'

Always, the people answered, 'Hi, town frien'!'

And Duke would come out of his van, dip his hand into his pocket and find loose change for kids.

*

Around Man-Man and Nenna now, the night was still alive with persistent fluttering and squeaks and chirps. All owls had gone silent, though. Man-Man and Nenna still stood with four eyes penetrating all sides of shadows and plain darkness. It was strange how after a long time in darkness they got to seeing better.

Unexpectedly Man-Man said, 'Did you hear that?'

Excitement electrified Nenna. 'No. Wha' was it?'

Man-Man whispered, 'Footsteps ... A twig did snap.'

Their breath stopped. They listened.

'You hear it again?'

Man-Man waited. Then his voice barely carried. 'No.'

Unbelievable, from a tree next to them, a bunch of coconuts of perhaps ten or twelve dropped and broke loose like a great pile of huge stones. A blast of gun deafened Nenna. Then panic!

A dim figure slid down smooth palm trunk like a man cut loose down a grease pole. And a flight now! All wild and crazy and mad! A tearing through scattered undergrowth like a mad wild horse. Another frightening gun blast! The figure fell with a terrible splash into the old irrigation canal, where there were few banana trees. It retrieved itself like a miracle and took off again with swift force. Racing feet thudded down, pounding through coconut-field darkness, swinging back some shrub branches. And, no holding them, Man-Man and Nenna raced behind hollering, 'Thief! Stop thief! Stop thief!'

They seemed to be getting closer. Then at the wire fence they heard the loud ripping cry of clothes torn. Then again the swift pounding feet raced away, along a narrow track on the adjoining land. And suddenly it was just Man-Man and Nenna panting their guts out.

'When – when he slide down the tree,' Nenna panted, 'I did t'ink he really dead.'

Her brother hissed with a wheezy giggle. And both collapsed, laughing helplessly.

'I did t'ink he really dead,' Nenna kept saying between gasps and fits.

Man-Man too tried to talk. 'No, man. No. A man – a man don't get dead like that.'

Getting themselves together, they realised how with the wizardry of the thief everything had happened almost in a flash. They'd even forgotten they carried a torch. Now, noticing the smell of gunpowder, they examined the barbed wire fence with their torchlight on. They lifted off the piece of pale blue material torn from the escaper's clothing. Almost circular, the torn-away clothing was bigger than the palm of a man's hand.

'Keep that,' Man-Man said. Nenna pushed the piece of material into her pocket.

They went along, holding torchlight on bush and under trees. They saw nothing unusual till Man-Man said, 'Look!' holding the light down on the foot-track. It was fresh blood on the grass. They looked carefully. They examined the blood-stained grass and stared at each other.

'Did you shoot him?' Nenna said, frightened.

'You t'ink mi crazy,' Man-Man protested. 'I not mad. I fired miles away from him.'

'Seems he hurt heself.'

'Seems he hurt heself.'

They saw more evidence of blood along the track. They walked more briskly, holding the torchlight along the banks of the track and at the root of trees.

They came out on to the village road. They shone the torchlight up and down but they saw nothing unusual. Man-Man suddenly admitted he should have checked round the root area of the tree that the thief had climbed.

They turned round and went back towards the plantation, trotting now, sometimes. True enough, their search produced a husking hoe, a small scythe and a large hessian sugar-bag with thirty-two husked coconuts. They collected up everything, took it all to the works-yard and woke up the headman of the estate.

It was two-thirty a.m. when they all woke up the District Constable and began their trek. The headman's old car spat, coughed and backfired its way up the winding hill road to Big-Walk's lonely hut. Even so they had to leave the car and walk twenty minutes.

Big-Walk's dog barked madly and alerted him that strangers approached. With his big and bare hairy chest and shoulders, Big-Walk came out in old shorts. Beside the leaning door of his hut he faced the party with his machete in hand, poised like a stick. The D.C. held his torch in the man's stern and serious face and told him why they were there. Big-Walk turned into his earth floor hut, lit his lantern and answered all police questions without any trouble at all.

The D.C. began checking. The log bed with mat, and no sheet or pillow, was warm enough to have been slept in all night. Big-Walk had a bandaged toe, but it was an old injury. His arms and legs and feet passed all the D.C.'s examination. Big-Walk was left as innocent.

Man-Man and Nenna's night in bed was short. At ten o'clock that morning D.C. Anderson called on them. He said a lot of doubts had come into his mind about Big-Walk. For one thing he wasn't satisfied Big-Walk's injury had not been given a very clever dose of treatment. In a small party with the D.C., Man-Man and Nenna went up to Big-Walk's place again and he was brought down arrested.

Villagers gathered in the square to see the bag of coconuts, picking scythe and husking hoe. Best of all they'd come to see Big-Walk on his way to lock-up. It was a day when everything eventful seemed happening in the village square. A truck unloading sparkling drinks had blocked the road and Duke waited in his van, with engine running, to get by.

D.C. Anderson was pleased to see Duke. Looking in from outside the window of Duke's van he instantly expressed his triumph of the day, which was getting handcuffs on Big-Walk. Remembering he wanted to discreetly fix a drink arrangement with Duke for later that evening, the D.C. came closer. He pushed his head in the far-side window. Then his voice halted. He was shocked. 'Wha' – wha' the devil you done to you'self, man?'

Duke grinned. Even his gold tooth was grim and paler-looking. Swiftly, sweat had broken out round Duke's forehead. But the D.C.'s eyes were drawn to the man's right hand, wrapped in a bloody bandage. 'My Gaad,' D.C. Anderson groaned, truly grief-stricken. 'Duke. Duke. You mean – you mean, say, it is you? You mean to say, it is you on coconut estate las' night? Stealin'?'

Duke did not answer. Sitting there in the cab of his gleaming red van, sweat merely poured from his face as if he got hotter and hotter, though it was not yet midday.

When Duke's lock-up van was opened and searched it revealed the other side of the man. There were the rough clothes, the gloves, the machete, the shirt with the hole that matched the torn out piece Nenna had given the D.C. Duke's van was loaded with coconuts, plantains, yams, and other things that could be explained as bought and paid for. But what about the built-in ice box, padded inside with sawdust? No words came from Duke to explain the contents of the ice box: the piles of stiff uncleaned pigs, goats, unplucked fowls, the sheep with its throat cut.

While Big-Walk had aroused the people's rage and noisy abuses, the new discovery about the town-man now stunned them to silence. Above all else, they'd truly admired how well Duke lived without slaving himself on the land.

The D.C. showed real impatience in front of the silent people. He roughly removed the handcuffs from Big-Walk and locked them on to Duke's wrists with a click of vengeance. It was hard to know whether the D.C. was sore because Big-Walk had got away again, or because he felt let down by Duke, or because he hated being deceived, or because of all those reasons.

Few people noticed the old man with a nervous nod who'd come up unhurriedly into the crowd. Big-Walk's dog friskily begged him for petting and licked his hand. It was Taata Raphael, the village bush doctor. He'd looked after the dog while Big-Walk had been in prison before.

Taata Raphael put his arm around Big-Walk. He took him into the rum bar and bought half a bottle of rum. The old man took up the rum, and walked slowly away with his arm around Big-Walk. He took his friend to his unpainted bungalow, surrounded by a vegetable garden with plantain trees, and coconut palm trees scattered about the yard land.

Though Nenna followed them, Taata Raphael hadn't noticed her. He and Big-Walk's backs were turned, going up the path of the yard. She called, asking if she could come. Taata looked round surprised. He put his arm around Nenna, saying, 'Of course you come to mi house. Buddy Willow long leg chile always welcome to mi house.'

The sun was bright and warm. Chickens scratched about the tropical yard. All sat on the open verandah. Big-Walk sat, sprawled on the bench. He kept looking round at Nenna suspiciously, yet as if he wanted to speak to her. Nenna said to him, 'Big-Walk. Why you t'ink people don't like you?'

Big-Walk swung his head round like a surprised bull, then hesitated. Looking at Nenna he sighed, then said, 'I not like them. Not like them. I me. I the way I is. I – I jus' me.'

'Know this, young Nenna Willow,' Taata Raphael said. 'Folks like when everybody else is like theyself. But the worl' not like that. An' folks not wise to that yet.'

Taata's wife, Naana Raphael, appeared and stopped the conversation. She took Nenna round to the kitchen and stuffed her up with peppery fried fish and bread and a mug of sorrel drink.

I had written the story. But that English teacher Mr Wills wasn't finished yet.

Mr Wills made me read the written version to my entire class, in my Jamaican voices.

3. Tukku-Tukku and Samson

ALL of the other boys call him 'Tukku-Tukku'. And this Tukku-Tukku boy doesn't like the name at all.

The name is used slanted, you see. It doesn't only mean he is little and fat; it's used to cut deeper, much deeper. It means he is a 'downgrow' boy, a 'spoilt-breed' who'll never grow, never be capable, never be anything besides a born spoiler. And in truth, he is dwarfed, smaller than all of us, though the same age.

You can understand why he will die first before he'll have the name 'Tukku-Tukku' fastened on him. But, you see, the boy who named him has an endless appetite for mischief. And *he* is tall and sturdy, his arms as good as new steel. He is clean looking like a young prince. He eats good food and sleeps in a clean, springed bed. He wears shoes to school. In class he always has the answers at the tip of his tongue and fingers. He's the best batsman in any cricket side at school. The boys love him. They call him 'Samson'.

It stands out a mile that Tukku-Tukku is different. He's everything Samson is not.

And Samson thinks he's really peculiar. Tukku-Tukku's face is seldom washed clean. He sleeps on the floor, is half starved, and has no shoes. Granny Tom, his guardian, cuts his hair. And just as she makes his little sister's dresses, the granny makes the clothes that droop and hang about on him. But mostly he is ragged. Most days he's a thickhead at school. No one has ever picked Tukku-Tukku for a cricket side. Yet, don't you ignore him altogether. He is sinewy. He is strong and tough. His pair of little pestle legs and bare feet know every village lane and bush track in the surrounding hills. Fresh air and wild fruit – and a full life of field, domestic and school work – seem to have developed something special in him.

So, man, it is Saturday mid-morning. A brilliant sun is up high. Birds are singing all round. Under the tall trees, only boys are at the spring for water.

Everybody knows something is going to happen. Samson is here.

You see, Samson doesn't carry water or wood or tend animals or work in fields or sweep the rooms of his house, like Tukku-Tukku does. His father is the local shopkeeper; also he has big banana and coconut fields and servants and hired hands. And Samson stays late at school studying; he seldom meets Tukku-Tukku on the school road. He goes to school last, swiftly on his bicycle. He often has to put himself out to meet Tukku-Tukku. Sometimes, though, the other boys have it all fixed up smartly, like this morning.

Samson starts his usual mock-petting of Tukku-Tukku, with his endearing nickname-calling. And he keeps obstructing Tukku-Tukku as if it's all accidental. Tukku-Tukku can't fill his bucket with water because of Samson. Then he gets pushed down into the water and the other boys go mad rolling about with laughter. Samson, too, can't help laughing. Tukku-Tukku rushes out and swings thumps into Samson.

This is a ping-pong exchange of blows now. But it isn't really a sport. It is a fight for death. The two boys buckle up together. Tukku-Tukku's toes grip trampled mud. Samson's shoes hold firmly.

Every vein in their bodies go stiff. You see that Tukku-Tukku's eyes have gone red. His lip has got puffy. His neck gets slipped under Samson's arm. Samson turns on strength like a vice on Tukku-Tukku's neck; he makes the boy look headless. And he drops his hand further down into his pocket and locks the neck-grip.

Tukku-Tukku can't breathe. He can't do anything with his hands. Pain has taken charge of him. Pain is ablaze in his head and body like wild fire. He cries a little moan like a puppy. The boys go silent. Samson lifts his arm away. Tukku-Tukku drops at his feet like a wet sugar bag.

Samson looks down on him. 'Ahright, bad breed? Satisfied now? You know now who's Samson an' who's Tukku-Tukku – an' who mus' get used to the name "Tukku-Tukku"? Then, bwoy, jus' accept an' shake my han'.' Samson extends his hand. 'Accept, bwoy – shake my han'.'

The defeated boy says nothing. He merely stays there half-lying on the ground, weakly rubbing his neck. In the heat of the sunlight, the lapping sounds of the stream and the varied songs of birds, his head aches. His lips feel weighted and peculiar. He gets up slowly. He goes. He stoops on the flat rock. He dips his bucket full in the pool of the stream. He lifts his bucketful on to his head and turns away. The whole gang breaks out into new jokes and cackles and giggles.

'Ahright, Tukks?'

'Coco-head bwoy, ahright?'

'Tell Granny Tom to trim your hair in darkness again tonight.'

'Yeh, yeh, yeh!'

'Yeh, yeh!'

'An' she to 'member to use her ole chemise for your nex' shirt.'

'O yeh, yeh, yeh!'

Samson speaks up loudly, 'Bwoys, you think we have the name branded on him now? You think we can call it success? Listenin', Tukk-Tukks?'

Loud voices answer, 'What you say then, Tukk-Tukks?'

'What you say, bwoy?'

'Don't walk away so fast, man.'

'Wait for us, man.'

'We goin' same way . . .'

With his bucketful on his head, the boy simply carries on home by himself.

Everything now points to the other odd thing about Tukku-Tukku's nature. Just as neither a beating from a teacher nor Samson ever makes him shed a tear, he never complains. He makes no complaints at all about anything to anybody. And in the same stolid way he never gives up.

Tukku-Tukku keeps it to himself how he will not be beaten. The boys make him get more determined to show them he's not just little. They laugh at him too much. On the road to school, to his field, anywhere they meet him, listen to what they mostly say. 'Tukku-Tukku, you're too small, man – know that? Eh, bwoy? Understan' yet you never goin' beat any ordinary somebody? Eh? Understan' yet you can't grow 'cause you turn out a bad breed? Come on, Tukk-Tukks, decide, man. Decide you're small. Decide an' be satisfied, man.' He can hardly go anywhere and not hear the odd boy shout, 'Decide yet, Tukk-Tukks?'

Only to himself the boy knows he's going to put an end to the name-calling and the insistence that he must admit he's nothing but small. And he comes to the decision that no one can help him better than something four-legged.

You see, Tukku-Tukku has heard about an old belief. He's heard that if you should lie down in a bull's warm all-night bed instantly it gets up, and remain there till the spot gets cold, when you stand and stretch you will find you have half of the animal's strength.

Tukku-Tukku rises early Sunday morning. He sets out and roams the cattle pasture wet with dew. He finds the bull still lying down, chewing its cud. Ragged little Tukku-Tukku creeps up behind the big animal and cracks his little whip. The bull jumps up, frightened.

Tukku-Tukku throws himself down and starts rolling crazily in the warm ground. All Tukku-Tukku remembers is the snorting of flared nostrils and finding himself on the bull's back, hanging on to its hump. And the animal is mad. It kicks and prances and carries him under a pimento-berry tree. Clever Tukku-Tukku grabs a branch and climbs up into the tree. The bull rages. He moos and bellows and digs up the ground with his hoof. But more good luck attends Tukku-Tukku. The bull's agitation brings down a cluster of cows. Because they stand there under the tree all angry and troubled they attract a passing villager, who rescues poor Tukku-Tukku.

The boy now tries out his strength. He lifts and throws things with all the actions of new and extravagant power. When walking he holds himself like a giant weightlifter. Once, he clenches his fist to thump the side of his little house but decides he won't wreck his own home. And, quite cleverly, he lets it get passed on to Samson that his fight with the bull arises out of his taking its strength away.

Listen to Samson to that? 'Yeh! O yeh! Then Tukk-Tukks will have to show me he carryin' half the bull's strength. Eh, boys?'

'Yeh, yeh!' they cry out in the village square.

One boy jumps about in mock agony. 'Now Tukku-Tukku make me start to ache. O how it hurt wait'n to see his mighty touch!'

Everybody laughs.

It's to turn out, too, that at the first opportunity, on the village road, Samson throws down his bicycle and uses one arm to put Tukku-Tukku on his back on the weedy banking. The boys, of course, almost die, how they roll about in laughter. Tukku-Tukku fights back, but only gets his neck trapped in the vice of Samson's neckhold again. He has to surrender. He has to walk away hearing the boys laughing and Samson saying, 'Tukk-Tukks, don't walk away like you're dead, man. You're not a ghost. You can well come an' shake my han' for your nice, nice name.'

On his mat on the floor before he falls asleep Tukku-Tukku now often imagines himself the tallest and strongest man in the village. And it is so real he can feel his clean, washed feet touching the opposite plain board-wall. In the field, weeding, he sometimes measures himself against a growing sucker at the root of a banana tree and says, 'You're my twin brodder. We goin' to grow tall-tall togedder.' Other times, in his backyard he imagines himself a boxer, and starts shadow boxing with all kinds of arms and feet antics. Yet, whether on the school road, in the cattle pasture, at mango, blackberry or guava picking, at the riverside or seaside, Samson goes on beating Tukku-Tukku all of ten times.

Tukku-Tukku now comes for a bucket of sea-water for his granny to use next day in her coconut-oil boiling. The sun is setting fiercely; a great patch of its light falls on the sea. Somewhat entranced by the sea and the light and the emptiness of the beach, Tukku-Tukku fills his bucket and leaves it on the sand. He walks dreamily and stands in the sandy basin of water. Waves roll in over the reef and keep refilling the basin. The water in the sea basin keeps rising up to his knees and lessening as the wave disappears.

He becomes engrossed with the working of the waves on his legs and the many sounds of the sea and the movements of some sea birds flying overhead.

Suddenly the gang of boys are there noisily on the sand beside him. He stands there in the water – not frightened to see them, but angry. Samson strips off his shirt promptly, to reveal himself in swim trunks. He pretends to be stepping past Tukku-Tukku's bucket of water, steps directly into it and hollers out in mock horror and apology at the terrible accident. The other boys holler too, in cackling laughter. Tukku-Tukku rushes out of the basin and tangles viciously with Samson.

Samson and Tukku-Tukku fight. They fight with the anger and the frenzied and determined movements one doesn't see in boys' fights. They fight like men. And this time it's Tukku-Tukku's arm that opens and swallows up Samson's head to its neck. The two boys push and roll about, Samson in Tukku-Tukku's hold, their heads and backs and elbows and body getting sandier and sandier. Tukku-Tukku gets himself in a sitting position and Samson can't move him anymore. Samson's eyes begin to go glassy. The gang pounce on Tukku-Tukku and release his grip; Samson falls away. For a few moments that seem ages every boy goes lost in silence.

Tukku-Tukku rises to his feet. 'Richard, fill back my bucket,' he says to Samson.

Samson, still on the sand, rolls his eyes towards Tukku-Tukku as if to say, you must be joking.

Tukku-Tukku is fiercer and more determined than anybody has ever seen him. 'Richard, fill back my bucket,' he repeats.

Samson gives him a little smile as if he wants him to be won over and forget everything.

Tukku-Tukku moves closer, his face even more rigid. 'Fill back my bucket, Richard.'

Samson sees the boys look at one another and then fix their eyes intensely on him. He realises he has seen something new in the face of everyone round him. He sees more than determined rage in Tukku-Tukku's face; he sees a new man. In each of his friends' faces he sees more than a sudden switch to unfriendliness, more than unexpected disapproval; he sees a final judgement.

Samson says nothing. He gets up slowly. He picks up the bucket from its side. He refills it in the basin and replaces it exactly where he stepped in it earlier.

Tukku-Tukku lifts his bucket on to his head and turns his back on the boys. And everything seems odd and miraculous. As they look at Tukku-Tukku walking away from them, quite simultaneously, it strikes them he has grown. Tukku-Tukku is tall as Samson. He's a big, big boy!

Now all of the gang tries to befriend Tukku-Tukku. As the boys go to school and about the village, their voices take on an odd sound, using Tukku-Tukku's proper name: Stephen.

It is strange how the battles of boys are soon forgotten. Yet one day Samson comes out with the old name 'Tukk-Tukks'; the boy only gives a smile in response to it. And today, as grown men, everybody calls Stephen Tukku-Tukku.

4. All Other Days Run Into Sunday

USUALLY I think I live in the poorest back-o'-wall bush-place. Yet, maybe, being myself, and a boy, in this Caribbean village here, helps to sharpen up Sunday happenings. So, I love Sundays. I'm not forgetting that dressing-up is a Sunday main-feature. And Sunday has best food. Those items help big to make Sunday a number one favourite. But, really, altogether, Sunday is different. I like how it's different.

Last Sunday something unSunday manages to get me involved. Me and my bigger brother are there walking to church. Up comes Harness riding a bicycle with Lanky on the crossbar and speeds through a muddy puddle and splashes up our clothes spotty. And you want to see and hear them. Hands on their hearts they plead, 'I so sorry! Sorry. It wuz accident. So-so accident! Can we tek yu an' wash yu whitedrill fo' yu?'

No need saying that with our white trousers and shirts being so messy, we just turn back home, all upset.

Later I decide, I'm going to enjoy next Sunday. It's the one day of the week when I like to think about things I like to think about. No teacher or parents to keep on bossing my head! I'm not going to let anybody or anything change my Sunday mood. Anything that doesn't belong to Sunday I'm going to shut out. Ignore them! Turn my back on them.

And today starts with its magic as usual. Everything today knows it is Sunday!

I wake in the middle of first chapel bell ringing. It's the 6 a.m. bell. It's not the bell of the church I attend; it's nearer home. Just about half-mile away the bell could be ringing in my own yard. The ringing surrounds the house. I wake in the ringing. In my half awakeness the morning is all a wonderful dream. First bell is the announcement, the declaration and proclamation – *today is Sunday*. No water-carrying. No wood-chopping. No school! Sounds of the church bell come like golden waves encircling me, specially, around my bed. It wakes me up now. A cock crows; another answers. I remember our yard-fence of blooming red hibiscus. I hug myself. In the waves of bell-ringing and cock-crowing I smell fresh beeswax floor polish, used to clean our room and the whole house yesterday. I remember – everything cooked today is special!

I hear, I feel, big brother's voice. His voice comes at me like regularly released arrows. I don't answer him. He keeps on and on jolting me, repeating my name. I think, 'Why doesn't he leave me alone! He'll be in bed till breakfast time and not a soul'll bother him.' I answer him. He turns his call on to my younger brother. All the same I don't get up.

I still lie down cosily and listen to the Sunday morning silence after the bell has stopped ringing.

I imagine the bell-ringer in his motortyre sandals walking away from the belfry. I know him. He'll go home and have Sunday breakfast on his own. His daughter has been dead a long time. A market truck of people overturned and dropped over a precipice and killed his daughter. His wife is dead too, not long after his daughter. I'm sad for remembering all this and I'm cross. It's Sunday.

I don't want any sadness and botheration to come into my Sunday mood.

I listen to the sea. Today the sea washes on to sandy shores and rock cliffs with a special Sunday sound of humility. Sea-sound today is hushed and humble.

My big brother begins repeating my name again. I answer him, not showing I'm cross. We respect this wakey-wakey brother because he's the eldest. Everybody knows our eldest brother has the worst luck in the house. No luck with book study. No luck with getting work. No luck with girlfriends. No tree he's called owner of bears sound fruit. And no animal he owns ever gets fat. I'm sure a curse is on him because he wakes up younger ones, then stays in bed himself.

I come out and see the morning's still not fully bright. But, red and bold, the sun has got up from the back of the sea. The new sun falls light like strange roads across some housetops and trees. Fowls have flown down from their roost. The cock runs about the yard chasing the hens. Me and little brother call the fowls together and scatter their mixed feed of coconut, corn and coco-head. Our pigs squeal for their food. Others will get up and help my little brother to feed them.

Somebody'll milk couple of goats in the yard. Somebody'll set off to milk the cow. By that time I'm well away in another pasture myself.

With a rope and a piece of blanket over my shoulder, my bare feet are good and wet in dewy grass. Birds fly about and make special carefree Sunday noises. Streaked with new sunlight, the morning is warm and moist and wonderful. I find our bay mare Clarabelle, feeding with others. I make a halter round her head, put the blanket on her back, climb on up and canter away.

Before I get to our house I run into a marvellous Sunday clattering of horses and mules that men and their sons are taking to the sea. My father, who is waiting, sees me coming with everybody. He mounts our mule and joins us down to the seaside, lined with coconut palm trees.

Boys and men sway in the warm sea, giving our animals a good Sunday scrub with bushy siroce vines. And we don't just scrub them. We get on their backs. We turn their heads to sea and give them a great swim out. Like ourselves, horses and mules love this. Like myself, they know this event means no work today. No work means it must be Sunday. And, by this time, even men and women who don't have work animals swarm down and make a big sea bathing flock in the water. And the scene is Sunday wonderful! It's like a village baptism of people and animals. Not surprising, truly, we all come out of the sea feeling baptised, brighter, more cheerful and more spirited. So, what happens?

The Sunday spirit is ready to turn irresponsible.

Once the noises of hooves cross the main road, all riders – even those leading another animal – shake them suddenly into a mad break-away. And a wild, reckless race is on, along the narrow, winding, stony dirt road. Yet every horse and mule expects it. Even Clarabelle and me are there in it. Bunched up or trailing, heads dipping, the animals hurry, making a mighty uproar with pounding hoofs, galloping round a bend, down a slope, through the stream across the road, up the rising, along the bit of level road, round other bend after bend, till Clarabelle turns into our yard abruptly, while others whisk by carrying on. I can never believe I'm still really there to dismount by myself, from the piece of blanket on her back. Oh how the terrible unSunday ways do creep in!

I dismount and tether the horse in great Sunday smells of home-roasted coffee brewing, breadfruit and yams being roasted and meats being fried, mixed in with other delicious promises. And Cousin J-J is talking to my mother.

Cousin J-J comes to our house on foot on Sunday mornings, instead of riding his donkey. From his shoulder bag that carries his towel and soap, he always gives my mother something – a special yam, some ripe plantains, vegetables, some coconuts, some seed plants, or – something else. Never sitting, always standing outside the kitchen doorway, Cousin J-J talks to my mother, in his slow, gentle, deep drawl of a voice. Then Cousin J-J carries on down the hillside at our backyard, down to the pool of our stream. There he has his special Sunday bath. Coming back he doesn't stop. He merely calls 'Bye-bye!' and he's gone.

The first most look-forward-to moment is really breakfast – all ready to begin! On ordinary days we eat out in the kitchen, which is a separate little building near the house. Today we eat in our little sitting-room. The table is covered with the bleached-out calico cloth that has embroidered flowers round the borders. It gets crowded with fried fish and fried liver, ackee-and-saltfish in coconut gravy, callalu, fried plantain, johnny cakes, roast breadfruit and different loaves of bread. There are big pots of chocolate and coffee. Usually at meal times, as a growing boy in competition with four brothers and a sister, I polish off my food to suddenly realise I'm still hungry, just ready to begin eating. Today is different. And with me and everybody sitting down together, I get a terrific feeling. I stay silent. I listen to everybody talking while eating. And I rise full.

We the children clear away breakfast things. One cuts another's hair somewhere in the yard. My mother is in the church choir. She sets about getting the dinner under way. When everything's under control, we know. My mother starts combing her hair and singing.

My mother sings very much the same Sunday songs on Sunday mornings getting ready for church. I love to hear her voice like this. I come out into the yard. The hibiscus blooms bright red round the yard. The sky is blue today with a much much softer blue. The sky is a Sunday sky. I listen to the Sunday singing of the nightingale on a high tree branch over in the big grassy pasture in front of our house. Cattle, horses, mules, donkeys – all crop the low grass leisurely. The swearing, whip-cracking cowman doesn't hustle and bustle them today.

My mother doesn't like us to hear the cowman's swearing. The cowman bawls out at the animals as if he couldn't leave alone any most terrible swear word and abuses. And the cowman reeks of stale rum-smell when he passes you. The cowman is a drunkard. He has a habit of going home late at night and falling in the river, and swearing loudly getting himself out. His wife drinks as much rum as he himself does. You hear them at home quarrelling and fighting often. They give each other shining black-eyes and bad bruises regularly.

I hear second chapel bell beginning to ring. It's a relief. I listen to the sounds coming and echoing. I realise everybody's pace is quickening indoors.

Everything begins to quicken gradually into a mad rush in our house. People going to church are passing and calling out 'Good marnin'! Good marnin'!' while we are getting dressed.

Not helping to lessen the pandemonium is the fact that some of us boys are very near in size to one another. Somebody mistakenly puts on a disagreeable brother's vest and there's a row. Somebody loses a button and there's big worry about getting it, sewn on. Somebody pinches somebody else's shoe laces, and there's an uproar.

Somebody sits washed in sweat, simply can't get his shoes on. During all this time men in light suits, women in hats with white and patterned frocks, and children dressed in varied colours are passing, carrying hymn books, Bibles and fans. Every now and then a group of the passers-by call out asking if my mother is ready.

Suddenly, I realise I have no shoes to put on. My shoes are still at the shoemaker's repair shop! My brother, who should have collected the shoes yesterday, has forgotten to tell they weren't ready. No shoes! I am out of my mind. So I say few words. Everybody is so appalled, so disgusted, that attack on the culprit brother is more than enough. I rush out of the house.

I run fifteen minutes to the shoemakers and fifteen minutes back. I come back sweating and panting. I see everybody has cleared off and gone to church, except, of course, my father, ticksing, oiling, combing and brushing down the horse. He doesn't go to church anyway, unless there's something really special. And then he usually rides.

I wash my feet again. I get dressed lightning-quick and I'm out on the road, out on my near three-mile walk to church.

I hurry along, alone, sweating. Luck would have it that, at the crossroads, where there's a rum-bar – though not open – non-church fellows are still there hanging round. My heart sinks.

I see that troublesome boy who's much older than me, that Harness-'n'-Bigtoe. He rushes up beside me and begins to walk with me. 'Harness' is called that because his clothes are usually so much rags, that his body is as much exposed as a harnessed horse or mule. Then, also, he has big feet with large big toes.

I don't dislike everything about 'Harness' at all. Harness is the best boy cricketer to watch batting, hitting sixes. Also, as a fielder, no ball passes his quick-quick long limbs. But, Harness smokes. He swears. He teases girls badly. And, last Sunday, Harness is the same one who made a puddle splash my clothes and caused me to turn back and miss church. I decide I will say nothing to Harness. Absolutely nothing!

Hear Harness to me, 'Bwoy. Dohn yu know yu frien'? I is yu frien'. Why yu wastin' time goin' church? Eh, bwoy? Dohn yu know Satan-life much sweet-sweet more dan sainty-sainty life. Yu can come wid we teday. Me an' Lanky an' Roadman an' Duds an' Duke an' everybody

currying' a goat down a Levelland. We goin'
drink up rum an' t'ing an' get cool swimmin'
in-a river. Come, bwoy. Come wid we. Yu goin'
come?'

I shake my head.

'Put down yu Bible in-a road, an' come wid we,
man,' Harness says. 'Once yu do it, it easy. Easy,
man!'

'Harness!' a voice yells.

'Yeh,' he answers loud-loud. I'm relieved, very
relieved, he turns round and goes, leaving me.

In church we sing and pray and settle down
with our eyes fixed upon the pulpit on the tall
Reverend with long arms and wide palms, giving
his sermon. I respect this man so much that he
frightens me. Whatever he says is true. It must be
true. Everybody loves him. Church is full. Now,
with a faraway look, fanning themselves, the
people are all subdued listening to the Reverend.
With his big voice he shouts and then speaks in a
whisper. He throws his arms wide open; he drops
them at his side. He talks bluntly; he hangs his
head over the pulpit and pleads.

I know that the Reverend is preaching about
the evil ways of men, and what he's saying is true.
But he makes everything so very urgent and it

bothers me that I should, but don't really, understand. I can't listen to him any more. I twist and turn. The day's hot. I wish I was under a tree where I could sleep without being seen by anyone. I begin to listen outside.

I hear the stillness of the day. The sound of the sea's even more mysterious now. There's no traffic about, nobody singing or whistling, nobody calling from hill to hill, nobody chopping wood or banging. This is the time of day for our man in the robe, and it is respected. The sound of his voice is the only sound that rings in all the open element. And he grips the pulpit, tugs against it. He turns his head here and there and questions, questions. Tears are flowing down some women's cheeks but nobody's answering. And it seems to me such a pity that nobody answers the Reverend. I remember how the congregation at the Pentecostal Church give *their* pastor a reply when *he* asks a question. Me and my friend went there one Sunday night and it was really lovely the way the people answered back.

When the Pastor said, 'Weren't you there at the cross, brothers and sisters?' everybody replied: 'Stood there, brother, stood there! Amen! Amen!'

'Brothers, sisters, aren't you still there at the foot of the cross?'

'Still there! Praise His name – still there!'

'Then, brothers and sisters, one day will His love not make you free?'

'Praise Him! Praise Him! Alleluia! Alleluia! Amen!'

'But aren't you tired and weary?'

'He restoreth, brother, restoreth my soul.'

'Who restoreth, restoreth your soul and my soul?'

'The Lord restoreth. Amen!'

'Lord, Lord, Lord, d'you hear what your children say? Children, speak – the Lord hears.'

'He restoreth, restoreth my soul.'

The Pastor then picked up the tambourine, rattled it, stepped down the aisle and the whole congregation began to rock and sing: 'Praise Him! Praise Him! Alleluia! Amen!'

Suddenly I'm jolted back to my church. Our congregation stand up to sing, startling me; I struggle to my feet. I begin to realize how much I could do with my dinner. But soon we're shuffling out of church, meeting the Reverend at the door for him to shake our hands. The grown-ups drift away, and we gather in the church again for our Sunday school. From my home, I alone stay for Sunday school. I'm a boy who doesn't really mind Sunday school but does take exception to having to wait till three o'clock for his dinner.

Going home again, hungry but happy, I walk alone in the hot afternoon, hearing the subdued Sunday sea-sounds, aware of the Sunday sky and settled Sunday mood.

I walk on along the main road. I come where the road is overhung with clustered banana and coconut trees on both sides. Unexpectedly, Harness comes out of Redground Lane. He surprises me but instantly starts talking and is quickly walking beside me. Before there is time to answer Harness, a car slows up and stops beside us. Obviously tourists, three white men are in the car.

With all three men looking at us, the driver says, 'We're looking for San-San Beach. Could you boys help us to find it?'

Instantly, Harness yells, 'Blackheart! Blackheart!' He turns in terror and flies, speeding off back up the lane like crazy, yelling, 'Blackheart! Blackheart Man them! Blackheart!'

I turn too in horror and panic and run. I run for dear life, racing behind Harness. The ragged boy disappears. But his voice echoes on and on in the Sunday quiet, 'Blackheart . . . ! Blackheart . . . ! Blackheart . . . !'

I stop in the clustered lane, panting, frightened out of my senses. I've come so close, so close-close, to being taken by Blackheart Men!

In pure dread and panic, every child is driven crazy by even the thought of being taken by 'Blackheart Men'! 'Blackheart Men' cut out your heart or take you away to do it!

I stand in the lane trembling, watching to see if I might be followed. I don't hear the car driven off. But I come back on to the main road timidly.

I look up and down the road. The car is really gone.

I feel lucky to be home. I've never come so close to Blackheart Men. Coming in last for Sunday dinner, I eat alone. I sit at the table thinking, yet not able to stop myself from shivering. My family lie down, sit about the house and yard, having their hot Sunday afternoon relaxing. I decide I'll say nothing about my incident. But I'm thinking about it so much! My great Sunday rice-'n'-peas with beefstew dinner goes eaten up, hardly making me taste its rice or peas or meat or rich-rich stew.

I leave the table. I come and sit with my mother and father and younger brother. I take off my shoes. I sit in the straight back chair and hear myself saying, 'Blackheart Men come try afta me!'

My little brother sitting on the floor leaps up. 'Wha' yu say? Wha'? Where it happen?'

'Comin' home – at Redground Lane.'

'How much white man them wuz in the car?'

'Three.'

'Three?'

'Yeh.'

'Is usually two or three togedda! Jesu Peace! How yu manage get 'way?'

I explain how it all has happened. Then I ask my parents, 'Is it only black children heart that Blackheart Men cut out to make medicine?'

'Yes!' my little brother says with great certainty.

'Long-long time now,' my father says, 'chil'run been fri't'n o' Black Heart Man. But I nevva know one child who get tek 'way so.'

'Nobody evva know one child who get carry off by any Blackheart Man,' my mother says.

'But everybody at school an' everywhere believe,' my little brother says. 'So it mus' be true. Blackheart Men catch black children. They tek them to foreign country and cut out they hearts to mek medicine.'

From bed, bench under tree and hammock, sister and all brothers come and join in, agreeing, 'You cahn say somet'n not in it.'

'Dohn worry, dohn worry one bit,' my father insists. 'Is all a made-up t'ing.'

'How it come get made up?' I ask. 'An' wha' it get made up from? How the scare did start?'

'That, my son, I dohn know. I jus' dohn know.'

My big brother points out that all the children around understand that Blackheart Men come either from England or America. We insist on my father to explain why that is so. My father can't explain. So because he can't explain he says that the men in the car who happen to stop me are only tourists. 'They only tourist. Only civilize people askin' the way.'

I remind my father I don't like running away from anybody. It's my way to stand up and talk. 'Why then I get so fri't'n of civilize white men? Why me a little boy dohn trus' them?'

My father can't make our worry disappear. Nobody understands why the name 'Blackheart Men' with its dread of being taken away by force might have come about on its own. Nobody thinks how much it all looks like an inherited dread. How it looks like the old terror when the first African people to the West Indies were captured, and brought over by force, to become helpless slaves, and now have descendants all over the Caribbean. The name Blackheart Men with its dread has happened all by itself. We stop talking about Blackheart Men.

Me and two brothers get dressed up again. We go 'walking out' visiting some cousins, where we are given pudding and lemonade and we talk and laugh. We stroll back home just before night comes down.

Going to bed I feel Sunday did begin fine, as usual, and ends up really well. It's in between that happenings from other days did show up. I begin to think how all other days run into Sunday.

5. The Mouth-organ Boys

I WANTED a mouth-organ, I wanted it more than anything else in the whole world. I told my mother. She kept ignoring me but I still wanted a mouth-organ badly.

I was only a boy. I didn't have a proper job. Going to school was like a job, but nobody paid me to go to school. Again I had to say to my mother, 'Mum, will you please buy a mouth-organ for me?'

It was the first time now, that my mother stood and answered me properly. Yet listen to what my mother said. 'What d'you want a mouth-organ for?'

'All the other boys have a mouth-organ, mam,' I told her.

'Why is that so important? You don't have to have something just because others have it.'

'They won't have me with them without a mouth-organ, mam,' I said.

'They'll soon change their minds, Delroy.'

'They won't, mam. They really won't. You don't know Wildo Harris. He never changes his mind. And he never lets any other boy change his mind either.'

'Delroy, I haven't got the time to argue with you. There's no money to buy a mouth-organ. I bought you new shoes and clothes for Independence Celebrations. Remember?'

'Yes, mam.'

'Well, money doesn't come on trees.'

'No, mam.' I had to agree.

'It's school-day. The sun won't stand still for you. Go and feed the fowls. Afterwards milk the goat. Then get yourself ready for school.'

She sent me off. I had to go and do my morning jobs.

Oh my mother never listened! She never understood anything. She always had reasons why she couldn't buy me something and it was no good wanting to talk to my dad. He always cleared off to work early.

All my friends had a mouth-organ, Wildo, Jim, Desmond, Len – everybody had one, except me. I couldn't go round with them now. They wouldn't let anybody go round with them without a mouth-organ. They were now 'The Mouth-organ Boys.' And we used to be all friends. I used to be their friend. We all used to play games together, and have fun together. Now they pushed me way.

'Delroy! Delroy!' my mother called.

I answered loudly. 'Yes, mam!'

'Why are you taking so long feeding the fowls?'

'Coming, mam.'

'Hurry up, Delroy.'

Delroy. Delroy. Always calling Delroy!

I milked the goat. I had breakfast. I quickly brushed my teeth. I washed my face and hands and legs. No time left and my mother said nothing about getting my mouth-organ. But my mother had time to grab my head and comb and brush my hair. She had time to wipe away toothpaste from my lip with her hand. I had to pull myself away and say, 'Good day, Mam.'

'Have a good day, Delroy,' she said, staring at me.

I ran all the way to school. I ran wondering if the Mouth-organ Boys would let me sit with them today. Yesterday they didn't sit next to me in class.

I was glad the boys came back. We all sat together as usual. But they teased me about not having a mouth-organ.

Our teacher, Mr Goodall, started writing on the blackboard. Everbody was whispering. And it got to everybody talking quite loudly. Mr Goodall could be really cross. Mr Goodall had big muscles. He had a moustache too. I would like to be like Mr Goodall when I grew up. But he could be really cross. Suddenly Mr Goodall turned round and all the talking stopped, except for the voice of Wildo Harris. Mr Goodall held the chalk in his hand and stared at Wildo Harris. He looked at Teacher and dried up. The whole class giggled.

Mr Goodall picked out Wildo Harris for a question. He stayed sitting and answered.

'Will you please stand up when you answer a question?' Mr Goodall said.

Wildo stood up and answered again. Mr Goodall ignored him and asked another question. Nobody answered. Mr Goodall pointed at me and called my name. I didn't know why he picked on me. I didn't know I knew the answer. I wanted to stand up slowly, to kill time. But I was there, standing. I gave an answer.

'That is correct,' Mr Goodall said.

I sat down. My forehead felt hot and sweaty, but I felt good. Then in schoolyard at recess time, Wildo joked about it. Listen to what he had to say: 'Delroy Brown isn't only a big head. Delroy Brown can answer questions with big mouth.'

'Yeh!' the gang roared, to tease me.

Then Wildo had to say, 'If only he could get a *mouth*-organ.' All the boys laughed and walked away.

I went home to lunch and as usual I came back quickly. Wildo and Jim and Desmond and Len were together, at the bench, under the palm tree. I went up to them. They were swapping mouth-organs, trying out each one. Everybody made sounds on each mouth-organ, and said something. I begged Len, I begged Desmond, I begged Jim, to let me try out their mouth-organs. I only wanted a blow. They just carried on making silly sounds on each other's mouth-organs. I begged Wildo to lend me his. He didn't even look at me.

I faced Wildo. I said, 'Look. I can do something different as a Mouth-organ Boy. Will you let me do something different?'

Boy, everybody was interested. Everybody looked at me.

'What different?' Wildo asked.

'I can play the comb,' I said.

'Oh, yeh,' Wildo said slowly.

'Want to hear it?' I asked. 'My dad taught me how to play it.'

'Yeh,' Wildo said. 'Let's hear it.' And not one boy smiled or anything. They just waited.

I took out my comb. I put my piece of tissue paper over it. I began to blow a tune on my comb and had to stop. The boys were laughing too much. They laughed so much they staggered about. Other children came up and laughed too. It was all silly, laughing at me.

I became angry. Anybody would get mad. I told them they could keep their silly Mouth-organ Boys business. I told them it only happened because Desmond's granny gave him a mouth-organ for his birthday. And it only caught on because Wildo went and got a mouth-organ too. I didn't sit with the boys in class that afternoon. I didn't care what the boys did.

I went home. I looked after my goats. Then I ate. I told my mum I was going for a walk. I went into the centre of town where I had a great surprise.

The boys were playing mouth-organs and dancing. They played and danced in the town square. Lots of kids followed the boys and danced around them.

It was great. All four boys had the name 'The Mouth-organ Boys' across their chests. It seemed they did the name themselves. They cut out big coloured letters for the words from newpapers and magazines. They gummed the letters down on a strip of brown paper, then they made a hole at each end of the paper. Next a string was pushed through the holes, so they could tie the names round them. The boys looked great. What a super name: 'The Mouth-organ Boys'! How could they do it without me!

'Hey, boys!' I shouted, and waved. 'Hey, boys!' They saw me. They jumped up more with a bigger act, but ignored me. I couldn't believe Wildo, Jim, Desmond and Len enjoyed themselves so much and didn't care about me.

I was sad, but I didn't follow them. I hung about the garden railings, watching. Suddenly I didn't want to watch any more. I went home slowly. It made me sick how I didn't have a mouth-organ. I didn't want to eat. I didn't want the lemonade and bun my mum gave me. I went to bed.

Mum thought I wasn't well. She came to see me. I didn't want any fussing about. I shut my eyes quickly. She didn't want to disturb me. She left me alone. I opened my eyes again.

If I could drive a truck I could buy loads of mouth-organs. If I was a fisherman I could buy a hundred mouth-organs. If I was an aeroplane pilot I could buy truck-loads of mouth-organs. I was thinking all those things and didn't know when I fell asleep.

Next day at school The Mouth-organ Boys sat with me. I didn't know why but we just sat together and joked a little bit. I felt good running home to lunch in the usual bright sunlight.

I ran back to school. The Mouth-organ Boys were under the palm tree, on the bench. I was really happy. They were really unhappy and cross and this was very strange.

Wildo grabbed me and held me tight. 'You thief!' he said.

The other boys came around me. 'Let's search him.' they said.

'No, no!' I said. 'No.'

'I've lost my mouth-organ and you have stolen it,' Wildo said.

'No,' I said. 'No.'

'What's bulging in your pocket, then?'

'It's mine,' I told them. 'It's mine.'

The boys held me. They took the mouth-organ from my pocket.

'It's mine,' I said. But I saw myself up to Headmaster. I saw myself getting caned. I saw myself disgraced.

Wildo held up the mouth-organ. 'Isn't this red mouth-organ mine?'

'Of course it is,' the boys said.

'It's mine,' I said. 'I got it at lunchtime.'

'Just at the right time, eh?,' Desmond said.

'Say you borrowed it,' Jim said.

'Say you were going to give it back,' Len said.

Oh, I had to get a mouth-organ just when Wildo lost his! 'My mother gave it to me at lunchtime,' I said.

'Well, come and tell Teacher,' Wildo said.

Bell rang. We hurried to our class. My head was aching. My hands were sweating. My mother would have to come to school, and I hated that.

Wildo told our teacher I stole his mouth-organ. It was no good telling Teacher it was mine, but I did. Wildo said his mouth-organ was exactly like that. And I didn't have a mouth-organ.

Mr Goodall went to his desk. And Mr Goodall brought back Wildo's grubby red mouth-organ. He said it was found on the floor.

How could Wildo compare his dirty red mouth-organ with my new, my beautiful, my shining clean mouth-organ? Mr Goodall made Wildo Harris say he was sorry.

Oh it was good. It was good to become one of 'The Mouth-organ Boys.'

6. Elias and the Mongoose

SCHOOL holidays were on, but it wasn't that
the boys were just mischief-hunting. They had
work to do. Holidays or no holidays, their spare
time was mostly spent helping parents. They
played their part in banana and coconut fields
and animal rearing. They helped to grow food
crops. They ran errands on foot and carried water
and wood. They had quite a hand in their
Caribbean village life, generally. So it wasn't
unusual for them to snatch a game and a lark
anywhere, any time, as opportunity cropped up.

It was afternoon, not a time you want to do
much in the heat. Adults hid and rested from the
sun. A goat and pig took cover in the cool of low
branches. A hen panted quietly on her nest. But

the boys were vigorously noisy, the whole gang.
With split pieces of tree-trunks tied into bundles
for firewood on their heads, they came from the
overgrown hibiscus lane. Bare-footed and in
ragged clothes, they entered the village road,
laughing and joking with each other.

Suddenly every boy went dead silent. At one
precise moment the whole gang saw Elias, the lame
boy they'd named 'Dancer'. Hushed and intent,
they drew closely together at the roadside. They
stared at him. Not knowing anything, Elias was
asleep, sitting on the ground, open-mouthed, back
against the ackee tree, a rash of perspiration on his
forehead. A bag was slung round his shoulder and
his pet mongoose, Mon-Mon, had its weasel face
peeping out of it, highlighting the gang's fascination.
The reddish brown and bush-tailed animal had a
collar round its neck; a string tied to the collar was
fixed somewhere round Dancer's waist.

Runt, the tough little fourteen-year-old who
looked no bigger than nine, giggled. Bigfellow
whispered, 'Shut up!' He went on tiptoe. He put
down his bundle of wood just inside Elias's yard.

The other boys quietly put down their bundles
of wood round Bigfellow's. All eyes were on Elias
again. The boys moved stealthily toward him.

Curled up beside his master, Lion, Elias' skinny and knock-kneed little mongrel, had been watching the suspect performance of the intruders. Lion gave a shrill yelp.

Elias opened his eyes. Instantly panic-stricken, he struggled to get up, clutching his mongoose bag. Effecting quick movement was not a facility he had. He merely flapped and sank. His undeveloped, mis-shapen and rubbery leg gave way under him.

Elias was a boy accepted as 'deformed'. The nature of his lameness was not known, at the time. To the boys Elias was simply as he was – peculiar, funny, fascinating. He couldn't read or write and didn't go to school. He didn't play games; he kept a mongoose. And, nicknamed 'Dancer', he had the very best name in the village. When he walked his dipping gait with reckless toss of head and shoulders was terrific entertainment.

His attempt to get away made a boy rush to grab him. Bigfellow tripped the boy. 'Leave him,' he said with an angry stare. And his action heightened suspense. Everyone knew Bigfellow's motives were anything but magnanimous. All controlled themselves, watching the lame boy gather himself up.

But then, with cajoling voices, with suppressed and open laughter, all the boys clustered and followed Elias. Hurrying, in his short trousers overlaid with patches and held up with string braces, he danced his strange dance, dipping, tossing. The boys cackled and begged, 'Go on, Dancer! Let go the latest moves, man. Dance, bwoy, dance!'

Like a stab, Elias heard the titter of his two younger sisters. Elsewhere behind him a fat hand grasped him round the neck. 'Wait, Dancer, man. Don't hurry. Don't hackle you'self so!' It was Bigfellow.

The gang laughed with helpless enjoyment.

'Is only the mongoose we want,' Bigfellow went on, 'thas all!'

'Noh! Noh! Noh!' Elias said. Arrested in his track he held his animal protectively against himself.

Bigfellow said, 'Now lis'n this bwoy. Jus' lis'n. This mister Dancer goin' on like he don't know somet'n wrong – somet'n suspicious bad – when a man start keepin' mongoose.'

The boys laughed out, their eyes shining.

'Make us move this little devil from you, Dancer man,' Runt said. 'It'll do you good, you know.'

'Yeh!' Everybody echoed. 'Yeh, bwoy, yeh!'

'Yeh, make us handle the beas', man,' Runt said.

'Noh! Noh! Noh!' Elias chanted.

Bigfellow said, 'Bwoys, you hear how Dancer say he not lett'n' go the mongoose? He beggin' us take it, ain't he?'

'Bwoy, you too stubborn,' Runt shouted.

'Noh!' Elias went on, desperately.

Bigfellow said, 'Ahright, Dancer, hear me. Bwoys, lis'n too. Man won't take the Espeut.' (The boys used the name 'Espeut', which had got stuck to the animal, but they didn't know it was the name of the first man who had introduced the mongoose to a Jamaican sugar plantation.) Bigfellow repeated, 'Man won't take the Espeut. We let dog take it. An' crack it up nicely. We sen' Runt to get Nip-Nip.'

That dog was the best devil of a mongoose killer. The boys echoed, 'Yeh!'

Elias bawled, 'Noh! Noh! Noh! . . .'

Bigfellow nodded with a signal of his head. Runt raced out of the yard. Elias began struggling desperately to get away. Overpowered, he could barely shield his Mon-Mon as he fell to the ground.

Some of the boys now had their feet on him weightily. Others clutched his clothes. Only Bigfellow on his knees actually touched his skin, gripping his neck. Elias well knew the boys regarded him as some evil thing and usually only touched him viciously.

They pooled ideas now, excitedly. When Runt come back we let Nip-Nip tear the Espeut out the bag an' crack him up. Yeh! Yeh! No. What then? We tie him up in the bag on a low branch an' let Nip-Nip leap up an' nip him to pieces. Yeh! No. No. We turn him loose in middle of the yard an' mek Nip-Nip collar him. Yeh! Yeh! Number one idea. Good. Yeh. We could form a wide circle round him an' keep him check if he try to run. Lis'n, man, lis'n this. We tek the Espeut . . .

Held there on the ground Elias could feel little Mon-Mon's heart pounding close to his own body. Having inherited the impulses of the hounded, the mongoose had tucked itself away from the moment Elias had become excited. In the grip of the boys and under their weight, Elias began to notice their pressure becoming more uncomfortable. He knew he somehow had Mon-Mon protected but feeling helpless and unjustly attacked he wanted to cry. He told himself if he hadn't been asleep he'd have heard the boys coming. He remembered that one day this same gang said they were going to baptise him and had thrown him in the river and left him. Another time they held him down on the roadbanking, stuffed his mouth with grass and exposed him to the gang. Why wouldn't they let him keep to himself! It flashed through his head how he spent his time watching butterflies and birds and dragonflies. He'd sit under the tree in the yard and watch people go by with their animals. He loved the way big animals moved their feet in rhythm, with heads bobbing. He loved the way dogs trotted sideways and stopped often to search for some unknown thing. He often went down to the beach, too, and watched waves chase each other and spent themselves on the sand. That was how he'd found his 'Lion'. A woman had come on the beach with a basket. She took out three puppies with stones tied to their necks and threw them in the sea and left. Waves brought back one puppy, with a string but no stone weight . . .

Suddenly, unbelievably, all heard the familiar, high-pitched voice of the big-built district constable. In his ordinary clothes, his battered-up

English trilby hat, and boots with donkey shoes on the heels, he was coming up in the yard. 'Bwoys, what you doin? What you rascals up to? Eh?'

The boys released Elias and begged him to go quickly. Elias stood his ground and complained bitterly to the policeman. As always when agitated, a slimy flow of saliva drivelled from the corner of his mouth. His eyes were angry. Veins stood out in his face and neck. But his words were slow. It seemed his words dragged way behind his thinking.

Bigfellow swiftly broke in and told the D.C. that the mongoose had got big. Very big. It was there in the bag the boy was hugging. The D.C. should look at it. He must have heard how neighbours were worried that it might get away and eat their eggs and their fowls. 'An' after all, sar, who would keep a mongoose 'cep' somebody like Dancer. You mus' admit is a queer t'ing keepin' a mongoose. You mus' admit, sar!'

The D.C. knew that nobody kept a mongoose. He smiled. All the boys burst out laughing and began to talk excitedly. Each one wanted to tell the constable about a mongoose who tried to kill off his people's fowls.

Elias suddenly looked the limit of both dread and despair. He moved and dipped his way hurriedly into his thatched cottage. He bolted the three doors and three windows and watched the proceedings in the yard through a chink at the edge of the closed front door. His heart thumped. Even the law wouldn't protect his mongoose! The D.C. sided with the boys! Even if it was nearer the truth that the D.C. only partly shared the gang's mischief – and that part of his mixed response was towards protecting Elias dutifully – Elias knew that the policeman sided wholly with the boys. He saw how he listened to them indulgently. And Elias strained to hear the boys' tales to the D.C. now about his oddities . . .

It was interesting that Elias had never shared most people's hatred of the mongoose. Elias always hoped a chased or hounded mongoose would do something very clever and beat men, boys and dogs. And it couldn't even be said he knew about the worthy phase of the mongoose's Caribbean history.

Elias didn't know the little long-bodied animal came from India originally. He had no idea it had been sought out and introduced to sugar plantations in the nineteenth century to do a job.

And the few animals had multiplied and unleashed destruction on the armies of rats who came out and attacked canefields nightly. But when the thriving race of mongoose had taken over the hills and lowlands completely they needed new food. They helped themselves busily to domestic poultry. Elias only knew that villagers would spend unlimited time following a trail, digging down mounds of stones, flattening walls, digging out trunks of rotten trees, to get at a mongoose. Whether it was because he wasn't able to join in or not, he never developed that hunting craze.

The day came when a mongoose had raided a neighbour's henhouse, and he listened to the outcry. He was sitting on a box in his yard. With five yelping dogs, shouting men and boys had swiftly set a hunt in progress.

A young, frightened and desperate mongoose had appeared beside him and hidden quickly under a small pile of dry leaves. Excited, he wondered what to do. He took off his shirt and quietly threw it over the hiding animal. He held it firmly. He realised no one had seen him. What a secret this was!

He'd picked up the box he'd been sitting on. He scrambled down the scrubby hillside of his backyard and stopped in the cave-like marl pit. It was very concealing. He'd often sat here, and sometimes slept. He'd put the box down; it had gaps in the sides for air. He caged the mongoose under the box and put his shirt and dry leaves over it. He had to have his shirt back. He went into his house and took out the rag stuffing of his pillow and put it over the mongoose's box; that was to smother the scent of the animal should a dog happen to come by. He had then covered the box with dead coconut branches.

Other low tree branches, crevices in rocks, odd places, all surrendered bird's and lizard's eggs for the new pet. Elias found out that the mongoose would also eat any bits and scraps of food from the kitchen. Collecting food for the animal gave him a new and exciting purpose; his secret warmed his heart. But it was watching the little fellow eat up eagerly what he had provided that gave Elias the special thrill. And there in his hidden cave, the mongoose began to eat off his hand and climb up on to his shoulder. The name 'Mon-Mon' dropped out of his mouth all on its own.

Elias couldn't help taking Mon-Mon out in the open yard to play with him. Then, the village boys got to hear . . .

Behind the locked door, Elias heard the D.C. tell the boys to go on home in his good-natured way. The boys picked up their bundles of wood but stopped and watched the constable till he disappeared in the opposite direction.

Elias's little sisters banged on the door. He opened it. They came in and told him it was silly to lock up the place in broad daylight. They re-opened the windows and doors themselves.

The boys had put down their wood again, at the roadside. They hung about the village road. Presently, Runt and Nip-Nip came racing towards them. It was all too late to act when Elias heard and saw everyone rushing towards his front door.

At once, the tough and swift fox-terrier type of a Nip-Nip found Elias under his granny's bed and started a commotion. Little Lion, crying and limping, departed sadly from under the bed. Then the real thing started.

Elias bawled, 'Noh! Noh! Noh! . . .'

Fangs bared with his wild mauling growl, the brutal Nip-Nip kept rushing on Elias, ripping away his clothes to get at the mongoose. The boys quickly cleared away Granny's bedclothes and mat. They took up the bed planks. They tried to pull away the bed but it was nailed down. Still bawling, Elias kept his face against the wall, his mongoose protected in front of him with his limbs and body. The dog had almost denuded him when his excited sisters announced, 'Granny! Granny comin'!'

'Wha'?'

'Yeh!'

'Yeh!'

'Sweet Saviour!'

To Bigfellow's command, Runt picked up his suddenly confused dog. Like thieves, the gang scattered down the hillside at the backyard.

Granny came in and put down her basket of vegetables in the little hut kitchen outside. She wiped her face with her large red handkerchief. She heard groaning. At her instant look of apprehension, her wide-eyed grand-daughters confessed that Bigfellow and Runt and Redman and Downgrow and Rufus and Daada and Minty had put Nip-Nip on Elias.

Granny dashed into the house. 'Jesas of Nazareth!' She turned round in new amazement. There at the doorway of the room was the devilish looking Nip-Nip, returned, surprised, confused, to see Granny. One bawl Granny gave at the dog sent him, tail lowered, speeding away.

Granny could not get over what had happened. She would not touch her dismantled bed. She would only see to the weeping Elias. With tears of rage in her own eyes she used iodine and dressed the broken flesh of his shoulder, his side, his buttocks and the scratches in his back. She'd known her two grand-daughters hated their brother. Their father had abandoned them all. Their mother worked as a domestic in the town. But, she, Granny was there. In the midst of them! And no man or girl or boy was going to stop her grandson keeping a little animal that gave him happiness.

In her great indignation, Granny summoned the parents and guardians of every boy concerned.

Runt's father arrived with a clipping of fur from Nip-Nip's coat and put it on the boy's bites, supposedly to stop possible madness or blood poisoning. The women fixed back and remade Granny's bed. Every boy of the gang was flogged, abused and disgraced. The little sisters were made to carry water from the spring for two days and fill every barrel, bucket, pan and vessel in the house.

In the pulpit on the Sunday the parson said, Jesus did not set a dog on a man who was lame;

he healed him. And though God did not expect ordinary mortals to be like Jesus he expected them to offer healing with kindness. But, persuasive as he was, the Reverend had not been to see Elias, let alone showed that he spared a thought for the little mongoose.

The dust of the trouble settled. The boys began to re-examine their mistake. They decided it was all bad luck that Granny returned when she did. They began plotting again about how to get the mongoose from Dancer without getting a beating.

7. The Pet, the Sea and Little Buddy

AFTERWARDS my father couldn't really stand up and count himself a man without blame. In the first place, Puppa had summed up the young horse and its liking for fun and games most approvingly. Over and over he'd said, 'See! A horse is jus' like a silly boy or an ordinary dog or a clever goat!' If Puppa had changed his mind about any of that I couldn't say. What I knew, as Puppa did, was that Misschief caused the biggest-ever incident at our usual custom of animal seabathing on Sunday mornings.

We were giving our work animals their usual Sunday morning sea bath. There, at our local bathing beach, our Caribbean Sea was dotted with the village group of us with our animals.

The round flame of sun had shortly come up from the edge of the sea. It was in the fresh sunrise we'd come into the water. And the thick clusters of coconut palm trees along the beach waved their long arched limbs about, at the new day, in the morning breeze. And the sun pitched long rays of new gold light across the sea and its white foam of rolling waves, and up over the hilly village of little cottages, with backyards of vegetable gardens, bare patches, a pig squealing for food, a cock crowing, a goat bleating, and a donkey braying.

We loved Sundays, my little brother Buddy and me – and not just for coming to the sea with our horses and mules. Children didn't carry water today, from the distant standing road pipe. Boys didn't chop wood. Everything had been done yesterday. And, truly, it was special and great to come out and ride and join the procession of other work animals, ridden and led, clattering down the stony village road, in the early morning. Coming along too while first church-bell rang was wonderful.

In the sea, standing beside our horses and mules, men and us two boys washing them, our black wet bodies gleamed brightly. Waves rocked us steadily and rolled on out against white sandbanks or against rocky cliffs further along the coast.

Straightaway the young horse, Misschief, began swimming about and wouldn't let Buddy or me wash her. As we got close to her she snatched her head away sharply and swam away and waited for us to come and try again.

'Jus' look at Misschief, playin', makin' the boys lose,' my father said. And smiling, stopping their wash, he and the other men held their bunch of siroce vines against their sea-splashed animals and watched us.

Pulling away, doing what she wanted to do, was freedom itself for Misschief. She still lived a carefree life. Misschief never carried a single person on her back, let alone a bunch of bananas. True, also, I'd sat on her back, but she'd promptly thrown me and turned round and looked at me. So that didn't count. And never to tell Puppa that, only us boys knew about it, anyway. Yet her freedom had been challenged. Only the Saturday before my father had started to break her in. Whether all that stirred a rebellion in the horse and connected to what was about to happen or not, Misschief was Puppa's favourite. And Puppa was really too much like an older boy.

Too often Puppa would take off his heavy work boots and, barefeet just as we were, played with us boys. He would spend whole evenings in the backyard trying to get the young horse to play with us. He would hold her, both arms round her neck, while my three brothers and other boys and myself lined up. He would then let her go; and the race between horse and boys would be on. He would rig up fences and we and Misschief would jump them together. With our two mongrels in it too, barking, the filly would race us up and down a gritty earth mound that we played on in the yard, while other children watched. And that wasn't all.

My father would let four, five or six of us boys line up the length of a cricket pitch away, facing him and Misschief. One of us would walk to them and let the horse take his cap off his head in her mouth. He would then walk back and join the line of us. Puppa would talk to the filly. She would walk calmly up and put the cap back on the right boy's head. But, the thing was, though Misschief was more of the big silly dog than the normal young horse, she showed signs of a malicious streak.

At an evening we would sit in the yard stringing green tobacco leaves or shelling dry corn, or anything like that, Misschief would creep up behind, snatch a hat from somebody's head, then canter all round the place with it in her mouth. Another time, because doors like the windows of our cedar-shingled bungalow were always open, you would look up and see Misschief clambering up the low verandah steps, to come and push her horse face in our livingroom.

A stronger wind had sprung up now. The coconut palm leaves swung about and rustled more vigorously. Higher waves rolled in. Puppa and the other men washed one animal after the next and took them and tethered them to coconut tree trunks.

I held Misschief under her bottom lip and waded away pulling her, and she followed, walking. Little Buddy jumped on to her wet back. 'Ahright, Misschief!' he said in triumph, kicking her in the sides. 'Let's see who's the better one now. Let's go, girl!'

I thought I really must have a ride too. But I first swam on to the deep. I saw that the horse followed with Buddy. She swam past me, nostrils flared snorting. Her mane and tail washed about, floating. I knew I was much out of my depth. I turned round towards shore. I expected Buddy and the horse to follow. But when I stood, panting, near the party of bathers and looked up, there was no Buddy to be cheered or envied for his ride.

Unbelievably horrified, I saw the little brother bobbing up and down on the tide, without bridle, without bit or reins, on the back of the young horse, heading out to sea. For a moment I watched, paralysed, I suppose, not believing my eyes, or somehow expecting to see him turn round swimming back. But I became panic-stricken.

'Puppa! Puppa!' I yelled. 'Buddy an' Misschief! Look! Look!' I realised no one had noticed. It all seemed so impossible. Little Buddy was so incredibly far so quickly, going away.

The faces of the men were frozen with horror and shock. 'My God!' one said.

'Saviour, Sweet Saviour!' another cried.

'Jesas! Jesas!' another voice echoed.

My father funnelled his mouth with his hands and boomed, 'Misschief! . . . Misschief! . . . Sweet girl, come back! Come back, girl!' Only lashing of waves against walls of cliffs, against sandy shore, and swinging rattles of palm leaves answered him.

Puppa could not swim. And by the time he'd decided to jump on the back of the dark mare other men were on their bellies swimming, or on the backs of their beasts going out.

I stood watching, numb. But I knew this spontaneous rescue bid was all hopeless. I could see the rescuers narrowed no distance at all on Little Buddy. They offered no hope whatsoever. Our Little Buddy, like a large floating bird, was sucked away, helpless, drawn with urgency, by some incredible power towards the horizon. As I expected, I saw the rescuers begin to turn back. They knew they could not catch Misschief. The tide seemed to have helped the doomed horse in such a fantastic way. Some of the men slid off the backs of their beasts and swam back beside them. The horses snorted and shook water from their eyes, ears and faces. The whole thing was completely unreal in this early Sunday sea. Surely it couldn't happen! It must be a dream!

'Jesas!' one of the men who stood with me said. 'Jesas, they perish! Save them, Lawd. Save them!'

But going across, as if they headed for the nearest point on the route of ships, horse and boy disappeared behind the little island of huge rock. We all ran out of the water. Would the waves throw them against the rock? Would they go down injured? We ran along the sand to see if they would appear on the other side of the rock.

Some dark sea birds with white bellies, who nested on the rock, suddenly flew up in panic and circled round in the air. A man naked to the waist had plunged many feet down from the rock and splashed. In his dive he disappeared but soon emerged in the new sunlight. He swam out swiftly toward the impulsive but innocent suicidal swimming horse.

'Is Taata-Joe!' voices cried. 'Is Taata-Joe! Mus' be Taata!'

Everybody knew the man who had eight children and saw him mostly in rags. He was the best known solitary fisherman of the village. He fished in all sorts of odd places at all sorts of odd times. He knew where fish and lobsters were. And, as swift as any lobster could swim backwards from any undercliff sea bed, Taata-Joe, with bare hands, would pull up the struggling bullet-eyed thing, thrashing its great claws about like an hopeless boxer. When Taata-Joe couldn't take home a full bag of seafood other men took home none.

Now, with arms wheeling overhead at first, then with steady breast strokes, he reached and caught Misschief by the underlip. He pulled her round.

Taata-Joe was soon to see that the young beast was exhausted. Whether due to its speed and rhythm being broken or its aim being thwarted, Misschief was suddenly drained of zest. A wave simply washed over her and the boy.

From the shore we could see they were in difficulty. Another wave rolled over them. Horse and boy emerged apart – that is apart from Taata-Joe. Still fastened to the horse who shook its head, Little Buddy gripped her mane. Taata-Joe had to toss himself like a desperate porpoise to recover Misschief before another big wave came.

'The reef! The reef!' the men began to shout with hand-funnelled mouths. 'Make fo' the reef! Taata, make fo' the reef!'

The rescuer gave no indication that he heard. But we saw him help my brother on to the reef. Then, with both hands holding the horse's head, he pulled her with all his force. And helped by a big wave the filly got on to the reef. She staggered uncertainly. She and Buddy stood weakly. The waves pushed them about. The water was up to Buddy's shoulders. Taata-Joe put an arm round the horse's neck and round Little Buddy and held them securely. A good stretch of deep, treacherous sea still divided them from land. I saw four other men appear on the reef. I didn't even see them swimming out.

Then, there were sudden, quick, thudding footsteps behind me. Coming from the lane of coconut trees, swiftly down the sandbank. It was my father and other men. They kicked up sand putting down the raft they carried. And in no time they'd floated it and were paddling out to sea, with me their passenger. I loved going out on this batoe because I knew it was unsinkable. Made out of light cottonwood logs it was terrific.

To get the horse on the batoe was the next task. She stood as if she knew she was totally incapable of moving even one leg voluntarily. Overtaken and overcome by her weaknesses, by the vast sea, by the clustered body of men, and the craft they tried to get her in, her large eyes had a fixed stare of enormous dread. She had to be practically lifted in. And it helped now that my father's best nature came out in his dealing with animals.

My father wasn't only the animal witchdoctor of our village who everybody called to their sick pig, goat, dog, donkey or any other. He also often bought animals who were next door death. He often brought home a ninety-nine per cent dead animal on his back from another village yard or down from the bush. Then for days he'd stay home treating it, feeding it with soft foods, talking to it in his special little voice till it recovered. Even vicious untamed animals had their way of responding to him doubtfully, like some uncertain child. Now that we moved slowly he talked to Misschief in his little girl's voice, and her apprehensive eyes began to blink sleepily.

With my father's incessant reassuring voice, with supporting hands given by myself and Taata-Joe, and somebody holding her tail and all, we brought Misschief to shore, standing in the batoe.

Unsure though she was of her unshod hooves, at first on the sand, and then on the hard brown earth again, she soon shook her whole body vigorously. It was as if she didn't only shake the feel of waves from her body but also the strange hands that had man-handled her. She looked up scornfully at the small crowd of new people who'd gathered, and pushed her way through them. But Little Buddy was in no such mood.

Standing in our big brother's old shorts for trunks, eyes held down, his dark body streaked with white lines and smudges of dried sea salt, Little Buddy answered no questions. He smiled at none of the bantering jokes of relief around him.

Out on the rock in the sea the white-bellied birds had now settled back. Unsmiling Little Buddy settled between my father's arms on the back of our mare. I rode our mule. And passing under the canopy of the coconut palms the party of us rode away. Misschief, without rider or rein, followed.

The sun was getting brighter and hotter every minute. We jogged along, the animals' hooves noisy on the road. The men had already begun insisting on their own version of what had happened.

8. Fanso and Granny-Flo

FANSO'S comings and goings and concerns were so well woven in with his granny's, it was hard to tell he had a big secret worry.

All the villagers had a big open worry – the drought that was on. For days it seemed it would rain, but the rain did not come.

The lands were cracked open and brittle. Food-crop leaves went into a deeper brown colour. Drought sucked the whole island dry. Grass in Jamaica was brown. Through all districts, the terrible dry-time had turned rivers, streams and ponds into near mud holes, trampled by hooves and human feet. Then, with rain merely hanging about, the air was impossibly hot and stifling.

Granny-Flo and Fanso were at work in their backyard. Surrounded by clusters of banana trees, scattered coconut-palms and spaces of white heat haze, they worked outside the kitchen doorway. They usually worked here, in the shade of the kitchen and the ackee tree, when their job was like today's. They shelled coconuts, milled them and boiled the milk into oil. Like many other district people, they produced their coconut-oil both for market and home use.

So, hair freshly plaited, bare arms with silver bangles, feet sandalled, and wearing an old blouse and long skirt, a piece of brown sugarbag sacking for apron, Granny-Flo sat breaking coconuts and pulling out the pieces.

Her blunt stumpy machete came down hard on a coconut gripped in her left hand. Cracking it, then opening it, she then let the coconut-water drain from the hollow inside into a bucket. With her strong slender knife she skilfully prised the white coconut kernel from its shell. Faster than Fanso could pick them up and mill them, she piled up the white pieces.

Fanso stood almost behind the squeaking wooden mill. He turned and turned the handle like mad. Turning the mill's grater-roller, cutting each coconut piece into white shreds caught underneath in a trough, Fanso milled as if he could never stop.

Granny-Flo rested down her short machete. 'Whoo!' she said. 'It so boilin' hot. Sweat runnin' in mi mouth. Jesus, Jesus – we need rain! All we need is rain, rain, rain!' In little groans she wiped her face with her large red patterned handkerchief that was already partly wet. She glanced upwards quickly. 'All the same, the sun gone high. City bus gone. Mus' nearly 'leven a'clock.' She cracked a coconut and then stopped again. 'Good thing is Friday, Fanso. Is not too bad keepin' you from half-day Friday school to help me.'

Fanso said nothing, though he'd slowed down his milling to listen. He quickened his work again then stopped thoughtfully. 'Granny-Flo,' he said.

Granny-Flo kept cracking a stone-hard brown nut. Still she groaned, telling she listened.

'Granny.'

Granny-Flo groaned again.

A piece of white coconut in his oily hand, Fanso stood erect, not looking at his granny. 'These days – I keep wonderin', mam – wonderin' – what – what my father looks like. How he look, mam. Is my father tall, short, fat, thin, black, brown or fairskin?'

Granny-Flo stopped. The question made her look paralysed. Silent, not moving, Granny-Flo stared ahead rigidly. Out in the village road, two dogs began to fight desperately. In their fighting terror, the dogs yapped and growl-barked in a frenzy. One yelped, running away, whimpering, with ear-splitting loudness.

In a sharp, flat voice, Granny-Flo said, 'You' father?'

'Yes, mam. Mi father.'

'You' father not worth talkin' 'bout.' She began breaking a nut again, not with any more weight or vicious chops. 'You mill you' coconut, Fanso. We don' have time to waste.'

Fanso hesitated. 'I was jus' thinkin', mam. We Independent now. Eight years now we an Independent nation. Prob'ly my father could help me.'

'Help you? You' father help you? Wha' he goin' do 'bout Independence? Wha' can a man like he do 'bout Independence, Fanso?'

'I don' know, mam. I don' know. I – I jus' think that maybe – maybe – through Independence my father could help me get better education. Or somethin'.'

'How would a man like he use Independence? Wha' he goin' find he know to do with it?'

Both Granny-Flo and Fanso waited on each other to speak.

Fanso said, 'Is my father stupid, mam? Or – is he jus' bad?'

'Ah Fanso, boy! Wha' make a man the way he is I cannot tell. Fo' now, Fanso – do, please, do you' millin'.' Granny wiped sweat from her face and began working again.

Fanso turned slowly and thoughtfully. He too began milling again. Granny-Flo bashed and broke nuts. She stopped and said, 'Fanso. Go. Please. Have a look at the pig. Go see it in good shade.'

Fanso walked from the mill. Fowls jumped up on the mill and began eating the shredded coconut hungrily from the trough. Granny-Flo shooed away relays of squawking yet stubborn fowls before Fanso returned. He said the pig kept cool under dry banana leaves at the root of the big mango tree.

'Jus' have a look at the "copper", Fanso please,' Granny said. 'See if the oil's cuttin'.'

Fanso stood beside the huge iron pot and looked at its grey-white liquid boiling furiously there in the backyard. 'It boilin' strong, man. An' the oil's floatin'.'

'Right-o. Since the oil's floatin' let the fire burn down. We won' push up the fire anymore.'

Fanso milled, his gusto making the noisy mill rock and squeak, but soon stopped to listen to his granny again. 'Whatever you got in you' head,' she said, 'remember, we have you, you' mother an' me – keepin' good health. We not the worst off. Thank God. You' mother may be away, scrubbin' people floor, washin' they clothes an' cookin' they food. But she work. We feed weself. We feed we small-stock. We pay we taxes. All we need is rain, rain, rain! Hot time need coolin' down bad-bad. Jesus!' Granny-Flo wiped her wet wrinkled face and arms and worked again.

At work, turning the rocking, squeaking mill, Fanso tried in his head to solve mysteries about his father. He didn't know for sure whether the man was alive or not. But he believed he was alive. All his life – thirteen years – he'd never seen his dad. And no true picture of him was in his head or anywhere to be seen. Fanso got his granny's attention and began questioning her again.

'You never worry 'bout him before. Why you worry 'bout him now?'

'I don' know, mam. I don' know. But – was I – was I a ugly baby? An' my father didn' like me?'

Granny-Flo chuckled. 'No, Son-Son Fanso. You never was a ugly child.'

'Is it my father didn' like a boy child?'

'I don' think so. You too young. You jus' too young to understan' how a man don' feel – don' feel – what a woman feel.'

Fanso stood in thought. 'Did Miss Sita do my father somethin' wrong, why the man jus' go away?'

'Do him wrong?'

'Yes, mam.'

'No. You' mother did you' father no wrong.'

'Then, what happened?'

Granny-Flo sighed. 'Son-Son Fanso. A man will mash up a woman an' they children. Fo' no reason whatsoever.'

'No reason?'

'No reason.'

'I sure won' do that when I grow up.'

'I hope you don't.'

'But – d'you think is true, mam, that because plenty black boys don' grow up with they father an' mother together is why we always so poor?'

Granny-Flo slowed up then stopped working. 'Whe' you get that? Whe' in goodness' name you get that?'

'Can't remember. But somebody did say that.'

'Then the somebody still need to say more. Still need to say how an' in what way I not treatin' you good.'

'I don' mean you don' treat me good. No, no. I don' mean that at all. I jus' mean that if you' puppa is aroun' more things could happen. Like – like how some children's parents in the district here can afford to have them wear shoes to school. An' can let them go on outing Up The Hill to old Fort in town. An' go away on return match with school's cricket team.'

'Mi Son-Son, you get on with you' millin' an' don' soun' so ungrateful. You jus' think how every time you' mother come from Morant Bay how she come loaded up with things fo' you.'

'But, mam, I never even wear long-trousers yet.'

'Fanso. Get on with work! You'll have to go up the top district huntin' water.'

Fanso milled on, milling more slowly, feeling ashamed for the first time that he had been abandoned by his father. He wondered how the other boys and girls at school saw him. And his teachers! Fanso felt a little frightened. Was this growing up? Was this what growing up meant? Discovering nasty things and worry?

At the end of his milling, Fanso was wet, sticky and uncomfortable. He took off his shirt. He set about emptying the trough of its shredded coconut, knowing, somehow, that something new was happening to him. He emptied the barrel of its water and brought it for the washing of the coconut shreds. He helped Granny-Flo washing and wringing the milk from the pile of oily shreds in the big wooden tub. Then Granny sent him off to the sea for a bucket of sea-water to go into the coconut-milk before it was put on to boil.

Granny-Flo herself turned and got on with the skimming of the boiled oil that had settled on top of the hot stock in the 'copper'.

Fanso came back with the sea-water. And with fire blazing under the 'second-pot' of coconut-milk, Granny had Fanso getting the donkey ready to go after water hunting. Donkey padded and fixed up with packsaddle and waterpans in two side hampers, Fanso rode out of the yard.

Fanso rode past their water-pipe standing at the side of the village road and didn't even look at it. Not a drop of water had come from it for weeks. He rode on past village houses, with people sitting out in yards fanning themselves. He turned off on to a rougher, rocky road and began passing people carrying waterpans on their heads, and sometimes on donkeys, horses or mules. When he came to Gush Rock, near a huge tree, a crowd of people was there.

Usually a gushing waterfall came from the mossy green rocks. Only a trickle came now. Fanso sat on the ground and waited his turn to fill his pans.

Other boys came up and talked to Fanso. He only listened, or pretended to listen. There was no joy in anything for Fanso. It was as if something new and all heavy had happened inside of him. He was a truly confused and unhappy boy. Something that made somebody a full person – something ordinary yet whole and big and joyful – had always been missing from his life. Yet he hadn't noticed.

To get back home before nightfall, Fanso was able to fill only one pan from the slowly trickling flow of water.

Both well ready for food, Fanso and his granny sat on wooden stools outside the kitchen doorway and had their evening meal. Fanso ate from his enamel plate, Granny Flo from her wooden bowl.

'City bus passin'.' As Granny said that, the bus-horn blared out over the countryside. Thoughts of a letter or some news or a visitor from the city bus always excited the village people. A sad longing in her voice, Granny-Flo went on, 'Wonder who get off the bus? Or who goin' get good news?'

Fanso took the lidded pan from the warm charcoal. He opened it and poured coconut-stock into two mugs. Strongly spiced with pimento berries, cinnamon and nutmeg, the warm and whitish coconut-cud had gone brown with all the locally made wet-sugar and molasses in it. And both Fanso and Granny-Flo were full of praises for the wonderful taste of the cud.

Holding her mug, Granny-Flo stood up, looking round, spotting heavy rain clouds. She jigged at the sudden sounds of distant thunder, and the way the time had darkened.

'Yehs!' Granny-Flo answered to somebody's call from the gateway.

Quickly, two village children – Tina and Ricky – came into the yard escorting a man dressed in white cap, colourful calypso shirt, whitedrill trousers and white shoes.

Tina said, 'Granny-Flo, the gentleman here say he know you, mam. We walk with him to bring him, from city bus.'

'Know me?' A deep questioning was all over Granny-Flo. 'Where you know me from, sar?'

'Look good, Mother Flo,' the man said.

'Lord above!' Granny said with shock. 'A devil resurrected!'

'No, Mother Flo. Passin', I jus' come off city bus. I stop to see you an' the boy.' He stepped up to Fanso. 'The children here who walk with me, say Fanso is you' name.'

Standing erect, with a straight stare into the man's face, Fanso nodded, speaking quietly, 'Yes. I'm Fanso.'

The man stretched out a greeting hand. 'I'm you' father – Mas Ossie, known as Bougsie.'

Fanso held the large hand in his own smaller one, all the time looking at the man with open-eyed astonishment. Belief and disbelief battling in his look seemed to say, 'Is this a king or a ghost?' His lips barely opened and whispered. 'Pleased to meet you, sar.'

Bougsie's face was lit up with pride. Here was his big, healthy, beautiful son he'd never seen. Still holding the boy's hand he turned to Granny-Flo. 'Mother Flo, what a way the boy get big. An' he so good lookin'.' Granny not answering, he went on. 'I tryin' figure out how ol' him is exactly.'

Fanso's eyelids flickered with shock at hearing his father could not remember his age. He looked down, embarrassed. Granny-Flo didn't help either. But, still smiling with pride, Bougsie said, 'Mother Flo. Remind me, noh. How –'

Granny-Flo cut the question and asked instead, 'Why you come here? Why you come here today, Ossie?'

The ways of his own mystery made Bougsie laugh. He let go of Fanso's hand and said, 'Maybe I passin' through. Maybe I jus' have to come special to see mi son.'

'You have more children, I hear,' Granny said.

He held up his hand with widened fingers to emphasise the count. 'Four more. Whole houseful.' He looked at Fanso again. 'Fanso, boy – I glad, glad to see you.' He suddenly pushed his hand into his pocket, came up with two ten-dollar notes and handed them to Fanso. 'Fo' you,' he said.

Fanso hesitated, looking at Granny-Flo.

'Don't touch it!' Granny said. 'Touch nothin' from him.'

Bougsie still held out the bank notes. 'Is fo' the boy . . . I sorry it so small . . . But – you know – things was never easy . . . Take it, Fanso.'

Angry and swift, Granny-Flo stepped forward and knocked the money out of the extended hand. 'I say don' give it. We don' want it. We don' want money well gone rotten!'

The two notes lay on the ground like strangely misplaced ornaments. Standing tensely erect and alert, Tina looked swiftly at her brother Ricky and back, to keep her eyes fixed on the notes. She made a little step forward and stopped, looking at the two adult faces back and again. She popped her eyes. Nervously she said, 'Can I – can I – take the money? Can mi mother have it?' Shoulders drawn up, taut, she waited in agony for an answer.

Bougsie said, 'I bring the money to give. If who is for don' want it, who want it might as well have it.'

The bare-footed and skinny-legged Tina pounced on the two ten-dollar notes like an incredible diving hawk. And, with smaller brother running behind her, Tina fled from the yard at record-breaking speed. Stunned, everybody was fixed in silence. The evening's darkness had increased dramatically. And before anyone spoke again, a great bang of thunder exploded. Flashes of lightning flitted and cracked the darkened sky with flame-like streaks. A world of rain broke free from the clouds. All three people moved with sudden speed.

Granny-Flo and Fanso dived into the kitchen, and came out strung with buckets and pans and pots. They put the vessels down quickly under the eaves of the house. Fanso shouted to Granny to get indoors while he dashed about picking up more bowls and pans, setting them to catch water.

Inside in the little hall-room, their sitting-room, Granny-Flo and Fanso panted and laughed at their frantic delight for the rain, while finding themselves beaten wet. In the midst of this, the fact of Bougsie's presence intruded. He was there, with them, standing, sheltering.

Granny's face changed to harsh and bitter. 'Not in my house, Ossie Brackwell,' she said. 'You not goin' shelter one minute more under mi roof! You hear me?'

Bougsie stared in disbelief. 'The rain comin', comin' down like crazy!' he said.

Sharp and rigid, Granny faced him. 'Don' talk. Don' bother talk. Jus' leave. Go, Ossie Brackwell! Go! Jus' go!'

Bougsie hesitated. He knew nobody refused giving shelter. All his instincts understood Granny couldn't really mean not to give him shelter.

'Get out!' she bawled.

Complete bitterness in the old woman's voice ran through him. In one swift moment he saw, felt and knew, he was originator and source of Granny's bitterness. He faced Elsita, Granny and Fanso and the strong relationship he abandoned. Neither his feelings, his sense of loyalty, nor his courage, had been strong enough to respond or give respect to the love and trust Granny-Flo's home had once given him. And forgetting it had not cleared the situation. A long stretch of time had not fixed things either. A devastating sense of his weakness and shame overwhelmed him.

Bougsie stepped to the doorway. The wild strings of rain were swinging and lashing down. He pulled up the collar of his short-sleeved sport shirt and stepped out. By the time he'd settled indifferently for slow strides along the village road, his pretty shirt and white clothes were all sodden, sticking to him like wet tissue paper.

Granny-Flo had slammed the door with a bang and bolted it. She stood, back against the door. She closed her eyes and bawled. 'He think we is like stone. Stone in the road! Like we have no feelin's. None whatsoever!'

Looking distant, Fanso stood, shattered. Something could have exploded in him. Fanso felt paralysed. He felt he could neither move nor speak.

Granny-Flo saw the strange look that had come over Fanso. Her rage softened. 'Boy,' she said, 'You don' know anythin'. So I wi' tell you. I will tell you. The man called you' father walk 'way from we when you' mother expectin' you. Say he goin' look fo' work. We did take him in. He the only man in the house. You' granfather dead an' gone. He goin' look fo' work, he say. You mother an' me give him we blessin'. Give him we blessin'. Eh, eh! Time go. Time go. Never a word. Never a message, a letter, a parcel or a penny. Till now. Till now. Thirteen years! You understan'? You understan'?'

Fanso heard only vague noises his granny's voice made. None of it came together as sense. Confusion made him feel everything a painful chaos. His strongest controlling feeling was disappointment. And his new-found father turned away in rain like a mangy dog.

And Granny was carrying on. 'Comin' here like that. Like all is well. Like he never did cause hurt an' host an' host o' bad feelin's. But – is how him is. Is how him is . . . Fanso, we do without him thirteen year. We can do without him now. An' forever.'

His voice a strange shrill, Fanso said, 'I don' know him. I don' know the man mi father. He come see me. He come see me. An' you drive him away. You treat him so bad. So very, very bad!' Fanso's eyes were filled with tears. His lips trembled. He sat down.

It was Granny's turn to be confused. 'Well! . . . Well!' she said looking round, realising they could hardly see each other. Darkness had come down. She went inside to light a lamp and saw that other doors and windows hadn't been closed. The floor and things were drenched with rain. She lit a lamp, bolted doors and windows and mopped water from the floor. It was strange that Fanso was there and didn't help.

Granny-Flo came with a lamp. She put it on the table and stood, looking at Fanso. She'd never seen Fanso thrown into such a lonely, rigid and angry distance. Suddenly her friend, helper, companion, was strangely cut off from her. She was stung with new hatred for Bougsie. She knew nothing she could say would help Fanso at the moment. She left the boy to himself.

Automatically, Granny-Flo went to pick up her clothes-patching basket, but then she changed her mind. She came back into the hall-room and collected up a basketful of unhusked red beans and two bowls. She settled everything down beside Fanso, including his bowl to shell beans in, as usual, and began her own shelling.

Fanso did not stir. In the silence, in the dim paraffin lamplight, Granny-Flo's shelled beans fell and rattled in the bottom of her empty bowl. Then the beans dropped quietly on others piled up. Outside, in total darkness, the wild rain beat the little cottage non-stop.

At last Granny-Flo said, 'Fanso, mi Son-Son – much I could tell you. But – all I'll say is, you father born bad. Bad, bad! He never was anythin' good.'

Fanso leapt up in agony and rage. 'How can you say that? How can you say that an' think you're good? How?'

Totally amazed, Granny-Flo stared at her grandson. 'Wha' you mean? You compare me with that – that – wo'tless man? Eh?'

'He is mi father, mam,' Fanso bawled. 'Mi father!'

'You' father?'

'Yes. Mi father.'

'Since when you come know "father", "father"? Since when?'

'Since I been thinkin' about him. An' since he came today. An' you hate him. You mus' hate me too.'

Granny-Flo was upset. 'Fanso. Wha' you say? Wha' you say? Me hate you? Me?'

'I sayin', first time I see mi father. First time, an' everythin' go wrong. An' I didn' even look at him properly.'

Granny-Flo could have cried. 'Fanso,' she said. 'All I do today is show mi feelin's. Show mi feelin's. I could do nothin' else.' She pleaded with Fanso to come back and sit down.

Fanso sat down and listened. His granny pointed out that he wasn't the only one who had longings. She had spent her life merely 'going from house to kitchen'. She'd never dressed in bride-white in church. She'd never worn a ring.

And, with her naked fingers, her one-daughter had come into the same bad luck.

Fanso suddenly said goodnight and went to bed.

Eyes wide open, Fanso lay on his back. His head buzzed with confusion. He remembered his father was tall, and dressed in white. He remembered the man's big hand holding on to him, holding his little hand, not wanting to let go. But he could not be sure of how the face looked. Fanso kept his mind strong, concentrating hard, to remember the exact face he'd seen today. But the face kept changing, becoming other people's.

He found himself imagining his father being most skilled at driving a car exactly right, dangerously. He felt sure that at playing cricket, his father was great. He wondered, could his father box? Could he swim? Did his father speak broken language or properly? Strange – he couldn't be sure. Yet he believed his father spoke properly, from what he remembered. He couldn't remember straight. The man arrived so unexpectedly. Too excited, he was overwhelmed. Only bits he could take in straight . . .

Granny-Flo prepared for bed. She was gnawed at by a particular torment. Had Ossie come to take away her grandson? Fanso was a big boy now. Most companionable to her. Most helpful. Doing well at school. Had the unfeeling man come to claim all that? Granny-Flo turned the lamp down low and fell into sleep.

A noise awakened her in a fright. It was Fanso, yelling, as if being strangled.

Fanso sobbed. Sitting up, legs hanging down from his narrow wooden bed, he sobbed, telling Granny-Flo how a bad-bad dream had frightened him.

In the dream, he said, he found himself on the beach playing cricket. He batted. And a man, who said he should call him Grandad, did the bowling. The man was good at stopping and catching. Other boys came and joined in, getting the ball sometimes from the sea. He hit the ball about. He ran up and down the sand for his runs. And everything changed.

He and Grandad were walking in the town, Port Antonio. Everything was great. He and Grandad had a good time buying things, eating jerk-pork and bread and ice-cream. Next thing, they were in total darkness in a tunnel and couldn't see or find each other.

They couldn't tell where each other was. They called each other desperately. Their voices echoed everywhere, mocking them, on and on. Then unexpectedly, they found themselves somewhere else, standing in the village square, outside the shops. He saw her, Granny-Flo, and waved happily and called her. Smiling, he looked round to introduce Grandad. And the man had changed horribly. He had no face. Horrible, horrible! His face was cleaned out and empty like a calabash bowl. The arms that came out of his sleeves were stumps with no hands. 'Horrible! Horrible!' Fanso said, sobbing.

Granny-Flo stroked his forehead. 'Never mind. Never mind. It wi' pass. It wi' pass. It wi' soon pass.'

She made the sign of the cross on Fanso's forehead and across his chest.

Next day, the rain had stopped. Branches of trees in the yard were twisted, disarranged and looked laden and weighed down. Like roads, rivers and ponds had been flooded. The sky was still overcast.

As usual, Fanso fed the chickens and pigs, milked two goats and chopped up some wood. Next should have been breakfast, then padding up of the donkey. But Fanso neither breakfasted nor brought in the donkey.

Inside the kitchen, a separate little building near the cottage, Granny-Flo sat, eating breakfast. She waited for Fanso. He had a special job to do because it was an unusual Saturday morning. They hadn't gone to the town market today. Neither were they going to the village market. To have a four-gallon tin of coconut-oil for market next week, and enough for home use, they would continue making oil all through to next Thursday. With market left out today, food had to be collected. Cousin Mackie had left foodstuffs in their hut, up at Overhill-Piece for Fanso to get.

Granny-Flo kept listening and looking up for Fanso. Finishing her breakfast, she got up and went in the house calling 'Fanso! Fanso! Where are you? Where are you, Fanso?' To her alarm, she saw a note on the hall-room table. The paper had been torn from Fanso's school exercise book. A message was written in pencil. She read it:

Dear Granny-Flo,

I have a father. Yet I have no father. He came to see me. I can't remember how his face looks. I didn't see how we looked like each other. And I don't have his address. I have to find my father, mam. I have to look

at my father properly. Somehow I have to get his
address. I have to know my brothers and sisters.

Your grandson,
Fanso.

Letting her hand holding the note in Fanso's writing fall at her side, the old lady's face aged more, pinched and glaring with shock. Where? Where will he go? Where can he go? she thought. He has only pennies as pocket money!

Granny-Flo looked at the open doorway. She almost threw herself, hurrying through it. She half ran out on to the village road and stood. Desperation all over her, she looked up and down the road. Nobody was anywhere. An urge triggered her to call the neighbours. Get them! Get them to get the District Constable to get the police station to find Fanso! But doubts followed. All would be shame heaped on her, that her grandson had run away from her. Then the pain of Fanso being handled by the police was too cutting to even think about.

Feeling very tired, very weary, Granny-Flo came back into the house. She remembered something Fanso's note said. The memory was like a stab. How could her Son-Son Fanso go on about father, father? Hadn't she been father and granny to him for thirteen years!

Granny-Flo dropped into her hard rocking chair. Tears came down her face. She wiped her face. More tears came running down. She sobbed, feeling alone. Completely alone! Despair came over the old lady, something like an ocean. She closed her eyes. She held her big red-patterned handkerchief to her face. Granny-Flo cried long and hard.

Half-mile from his house, Fanso waited at the bus-stop. Walled by towering coconut palm trees on each side of the road, he'd joined a small crowd of other village people. Worried, impatient, expectant, Fanso didn't want to talk to anybody. But neither could he stand still.

Fanso looked everyone up and down who came and joined the waiting passengers, although he knew the person. It was as if he wanted to say to everybody, 'Have you seen my father? Do you know where he went last night out of the rain? Any idea where I could find him this morning? Any idea at all?' Fanso held his head down, knowing he must ask nothing, must arouse no suspicion. Somebody he respected – somebody bigger and stronger and able to get help – might hold him and drag him back to his granny. So, wondering, he kept his watch and speculation a secret. Without anyone knowing why, he kept his searching gaze on every donkey, horse, mule or bicycle rider who came towards the bus-stop and passed. He strained to see every person in every occasional car or truck that passed.

Then Fanso realised he had no idea what he'd do when he got on the bus – that went fourteen miles away to his parish town Port Antonio. From there he had another sixty miles to do to get to the city Kingston. He knew his father lived in Kingston. He didn't have enough money to pay to get anywhere. Boys often tried to ride for nothing. But conductors took spiteful pleasure in putting a boy off miles from anywhere. He couldn't just walk, either. His granny might send the District Constable after him, who'd find him easily. . . .

In its usual fanfare of loud horn-blowing, the big, creaky old city bus groaned up and stopped. Fanso was instantly anxious to get himself on it. But – in the stir and chatter of people getting off and getting on – to his horror, his mother stepped down from the bus, asking someone to hand down her two bankra baskets.

Instantly, Fanso tried to disguise himself. He was about to step forward and up, nippily inside. Full of surprise, standing tall in floral-patterned frock and red earrings, Fanso's mother put her hand against his cheek and said, 'I glad to see you. I didn' sen' message to say I comin'. How did you know to come an' meet me? How did you know?'

Fanso held his head down. 'I didn' know. Good mornin', mam.' And Fanso didn't even look at the bus anymore. In its showy fanfare of departure, the bus moved off with its loudest engine roar and longest piece of horn-blowing.

Elsita stood, examining her son. 'Fanso. You dressed up. You didn' know I was comin'. You didn' come to meet me. Where you did a-go? An' dressed up an' all! To where?'

'I can't tell you, Miss Sita.'

'What? You can't tell you' mother where you were goin'?'

'No, mam.'

'Fanso. Wha's happenin'?'

'Granny-Flo wi' tell you.'

Puzzled, looking at her son, Elsita said, 'Okay. Awright. We goin' home straight, you know.'

'Yes, mam.'

In the clammy and overcast morning, they began to walk. Fanso carried the heavier-lidded basket on his head. Elsita carried the other at the end of one arm. Answering his mother's questions as he felt like it, Fanso talked little.

Vaguely, distantly, Granny-Flo heard a voice. She opened her eyes. Someone stood at the doorway saying, 'Mummah. Mummah. Wha's matter?'

Elsita crouched beside the rocking chair. Granny-Flo embraced her daughter. 'Sita. Sita. God sen' you. Oh, mi one-child, God sen' you.'

Elsita looked into her mother's face. 'Why you been cryin', mam? Why you did a-cry?'

'Sita. Everythin' is terrible.'

'Terrible? Why?'

'Sita. You' son – you' son Fanso – gone!'

'Wha' you mean Fanso gone?' Elsita looked round. 'Fanso's here. We jus' come in together.'

'Wha' you say?' Granny-Flo turned and saw Fanso. In disbelief she cried out, 'Whai-o! Whai-o! Him is here. Fanso. Where did you go?' She turned to Elsita. 'Sita. Did the boy tell you he try to run away?'

'Run away?'

With Granny-Flo excitedly explaining the trouble that had overtaken them, the mother and daughter sat down in the hall-room. Elsita kept eyeing Fanso, wanting him to say something. Fanso stood in silence at the window, leaning against the wall. But Elsita and Granny-Flo interrogated him, reprimanded him, showered him with their rage and disgust, and emphasised the many ways that both of them had been good to him.

Elsita picked up Fanso's note, read it, then stood there looking lost. Her mother kept her eyes on her and thought how lovely her tall daughter looked, in her red earrings and her fresh and cool floral frock. Then she began remembering their shared disappointments, pains and frightening situations together.

'Fanso,' Elsita said. 'I jus' come all the way from my work at Morant Bay to spen' two days with you. An' look at the news you provide fo' you' mother. You not ashamed?'

'I pleased to see you, mam,' Fanso said.

'Then it not a big pity I have to hear you try to leave home?'

Fanso held his head down, remembering that of all his granny and mother had said, nothing had been said about his wanting to see his father and sisters and brothers, all of whom he'd just discovered.

'Eh, Fanso?' his mother insisted.

'It's a pity, mam.'

'An' I don' yet hear you say you sorry, you know. An' that you not goin' do it again.'

'I sorry.'

'An' what about the rest of it?'

'I not goin' do it again.'

Elsita went silent, then said, 'Bring the big bankra over to me, please.'

Elsita opened the lidded basket. From it she unwrapped a pair of trousers. She gave Fanso the trousers and told him to try them on. Fanso put on his first pair of long-trousers and couldn't believe his luck.

Excited, tickled, smiling – a changed boy – Fanso said, 'It's whitedrill!'

'Yes. Is whitedrill,' his mother said.

A smile on his face, Fanso went on, 'You didn' happen to bring a cricket bat as well?'

'No. Not this time.'

'So there's hope?'

'Never give up hope, I say.'

Feeling good in his long-trousers, Fanso embraced his mother. 'The trousers great, mam. Really great! Thanks.'

Nothing more was said about his father, about the written note he left or about his disappearance that morning.

Though it had seemed it would rain again, later the sun came out brightly.

Fanso and Elsita took the donkey up to Overhill-Piece.

The hut on Granny-Flo's land stood there, surrounded by coconut palms, avocado, banana and nutmeg trees and random clusters of food plants.

Fanso and his mother worked pleasantly together. They brought out the things from the hut. They had loaded the donkey with yams, pumpkins, plaintains, cabbages, cho-chos, okras, other vegetables and pieces of sugar-cane, when Fanso confronted Elsita. He began light-heartedly, as if somehow he knew he had a chance of winning her over. 'So, Miss Sita,' he said, 'mi father come drop big surprise on we. With no warnin', the man come look me up. Come off city bus. Jus' like that. Did you hear about it, mam?'

Elsita was all flat and cool. 'Yes. I hear.'

Fanso went on working and chatting, giving details of the impact the man had made on him. 'Then, mam,' he said, 'it all comes out I have brothers an' sisters. Did you know that, Miss Sita? Did you know I have brothers an' sisters?'

'I hear about it.'

'You did hear about it? Long time?'

'Some time back.'

Fanso stopped working. He looked at his mother across the donkey back, still packing her hamper, not looking at him. 'Well, mam – well, mam – I want to know them. I am goin' to get to know them?'

Elsita sighed. 'One day you will, Fanso. You will, I'm sure. You turnin' man everyday more an' more.'

Fanso couldn't believe what he heard. 'But I want to know my brothers an' sisters now. Long, long before I turn big-man.'

Elsita's patience ran out. Her face twisted, she bawled, 'I'm sick of you' talk, talk, talk! Come on. Let we get on. An' finish loadin' the donkey! I want to get back home.'

The boy looked at his mother. He turned. His cheerfulness gone, his pace slowed, his shoulders drooping, he brought a small bunch of bananas out of the hut, dragging it.

9. The Banana Tree

IN THE hours the hurricane stayed, its presence made everybody older. It made Mr Bass see that not only people and animals and certain valuables were of most importance to be saved.

From its very build-up the hurricane meant to show it was merciless, unstoppable, and with its might it changed landscapes.

All day the Jamaican sun didn't come out. Then, ten minutes before, there was a swift shower of rain that raced by and was gone like some urgent messenger-rush of wind. And, again, everything went back to that quiet, that unnatural quiet. It was as if trees crouched quietly in fear. As if, too, birds knew they should shut up. A thick and low black cloud had covered the sky and shadowed everywhere, and made it seem like night was coming on. And the cloud deepened. Its deepening spread more and more over the full stretch of the sea.

The doom-laden afternoon had the atmosphere of Judgement Day for everybody in all the districts about. Everybody knew the hour of disaster was near. Warnings printed in bold lettering had been put up at post offices, police stations, schoolyard entrances and in clear view on shop walls in village squares.

Carrying children and belongings, people hurried in files and in scattered groups, headed for the big, strong and safe community buildings. In Canerise Village, we headed for the schoolroom. Loaded with bags and cases, with bundles and lidded baskets, individuals carrying or leading an animal, parents shrieking for children to stay at their heels, we arrived there. And, looking round, anyone would think the whole of Canerise was here in this vast super barn of a noisy chattering schoolroom.

With violent gusts and squalls the storm broke. Great rushes, huge bulky rushes, of wind struck the building in heavy repeated thuds, shaking it over and over, and carrying on.

Families were huddled together on the floor. People sang, sitting on benches, desks, anywhere there was room. Some people knelt in loud prayer. Among the refugees' noises a goat bleated, a hen fluttered or cackled, a dog whined.

Mr Jetro Bass was sitting on a soap-box. His broad back leaned on the blackboard against the wall. Mrs Imogene Bass, largely pregnant, looked a midget beside him. Their children were sitting on the floor. The eldest boy, Gustus, sat farthest from his father. Altogether, the children's heads made seven different levels of height around the parents. Mr Bass forced a reassuring smile. His toothbrush moustache moved about a bit as he said, 'The storm's bad, chil'run. Really bad. But it'll blow off. It'll spen' itself out. It'll kill itself.'

Except for Gustus, all the faces of the children turned up with subdued fear and looked at their father as he spoke.

'Das true wha' Pappy say,' Mrs Bass said. 'The good Lord wohn gi' we more than we can bear.'

Mr Bass looked at Gustus. He stretched fully through the sitting children and put a lumpy, blistery hand – though a huge hand – on the boy's head, almost covering it. The boy's clear brown eyes looked straight and unblinkingly into his father's face. 'Wha's the matter, bwoy?' his dad asked.

He shook his head. 'Nothin', Pappy.'

'Wha' mek you say "not'n"? I sure somet'in' bodder you, Gustus. You not a bwoy who fright'n easy. Is not the hurricane wha' bodder you? Tell Pappy.'

'Is nothin'.'

'You're a big bwoy now. Gustus – you nearly thirteen. You strong. You very useful fo' you' age. You good as mi right han'. I depen' on you. But this afternoon – earlier – in the rush, when we so well push to move befo' storm brok', you couldn' rememba a t'ing! Not one t'ing! Why so? Wha' on you' mind? You 'arbourin' t'ings from me, Gustus?'

Gustus opened his mouth to speak, but closed it again. He knew his father was proud of how well he had grown. To strengthen him he had always given him 'last milk' straight from the cow in the mornings. He was thankful. But to him his strength was only proven in the number of wickets he could take for his cricket team. The boy's lips trembled. What's the good of tellin' when pappy don' like cricket. He only get vex an' say it's Satan's game for idle hands! He twisted his head and looked away. 'I'm 'arbourin' nothin', Pappy.'

'Gustus . . .'

At that moment a man called, 'Mr Bass!' He came up quickly. 'Got a hymn book, Mr Bass? We want you to lead us singing.

The people were sitting with bowed heads, humming a song. As the repressed singing grew louder and louder it sounded mournful in the room. Mr Bass shuffled, looking round as if he wished to back out of the suggestion. But his rich voice and singing-leadership were too famous. Mrs Bass already had the hymn book in her hand and she pushed it on her husband. He took it, and began turning the leaves as he moved towards the centre of the room.

Immediately, Mr Bass was surrounded. He started with a resounding chant over the heads of everybody. 'Abide wid me, fast fall da eventide . . .' He joined the singing, but broke off to recite the other line. 'Da darkness deepen, Lord wid me abide . . .' Again, before the last long-drawn note faded from the deeply stirred voices, Mr Bass intoned musically, 'When odder 'elpers fail, and comfats flee . . .'

In this manner he fired inspiration into the singing of hymn after hymn. The congregation swelled their throats and their mixed voices filled the room, pleading to heaven from the depths of their hearts. But the wind outside mocked viciously. It screamed. It whistled. It smashed everywhere up.

Mrs Bass had tightly closed her eyes, singing and swaying in the centre of the children who nestled round her. But Gustus was by himself. He had his elbows on his knees and his hands blocking his ears. He had his own worries.

What's the good of Pappy asking all those questions when he treat him so bad. He's the only one in the family without a pair of shoes! Because he's a big boy he dohn need anythin' an' must do all the work. He can't stay at school in the evenings an' play cricket because there's work to do at home. He can't have no outings with the other children because he has no shoes. An' now when he was to sell his bunch of bananas an' buy shoes so he can go out with his cricket team, the hurricane is going to blow it down.

It was true: the root of the banana was his 'navel string'. After his birth the umbilical cord was dressed with castor oil and sprinkled with nutmeg and buried, with the banana tree planted over it for him. When he was nine days old the

Nana midwife had taken him out into the open for the first time. She had held the infant proudly and walked the twenty-five yards that separated the house from the kitchen, and at the back showed him his tree. ''Memba w'en you grow up,' her toothless mouth had said, 'It's you nable strings feedin' you tree, the same way it feed you from you mudder.'

Refuse from the kitchen made the plant flourish out of all proportion. But the rich soil around it was loose. Each time the tree gave a shoot, the bunch would be too heavy for the soil to support; so it crashed to the ground, crushing the tender fruit. This time, determined that his banana must reach the market, Gustus had supported his tree with eight props. And watching it night and morning it had become very close to him. Often he had seriously thought of moving his bed to its root.

Muffled cries, and the sound of blowing noses, now mixed with the singing. Delayed impact of the disaster was happening. Sobbing was everywhere. Quickly the atmosphere became sodden with the wave of weeping outbursts. Mrs Bass's pregnant belly heaved. Her younger children were upset and cried, 'Mammy, mammy, mammy . . .'

Realising that his family, too, was overwhelmed by the surrounding calamity, Mr Bass bustled over to them. Because their respect for him bordered fear, his presence quietened all immediately. He looked round. 'Where's Gustus! Imogene . . . where's Gustus!'

'He was 'ere, Pappy,' she replied, drying her eyes. 'I dohn know when he get up.'

Briskly, Mr Bass began combing the schoolroom to find his boy. He asked; no one had seen Gustus. He called. There was no answer. He tottered, lifting his heavy boots over heads, fighting his way to the jalousie. He opened it and his eyes gleamed up and down the road, but saw nothing of him. In despair Mr Bass gave one last thunderous shout: 'Gustus!' Only the wind sneered.

By this time Gustus was half-way on the mile journey to their house. The lone figure in the raging wind and shin-deep road-flood was tugging, snapping and pitching branches out of his path. His shirt was fluttering from his back like a boat-sail. And a leaf was fastened to his cheek. But the belligerent wind was merciless. It bellowed into his ears and drummed a deafening commotion. As he grimaced and covered his ears he was forcefully slapped against a coconut tree trunk that laid across the road.

When his eyes opened, his round face was turned up to a festered sky. Above the tormented trees a zinc sheet writhed, twisted and somersaulted in the tempestuous flurry. Leaves of all shapes and sizes were whirling and diving like attackers around the zinc sheet. As Gustus turned to get up, a bullet-drop of rain struck his temple. He shook his head, held grimly to the tree trunk and struggled to his feet.

Where the road was clear, he edged along the bank. Once, when the wind staggered him, he recovered with his legs wide apart. Angrily, he stretched out his hands with clenched fists and shouted: 'I almos' hol' you dat time . . . come solid like dat again an' we fight like man an' man!'

When Gustus approached the river he had to cross, it was flooded and blocked beyond recognition. Pressing his chest against the gritty road-bank the boy closed his weary eyes on the brink of the spating river. The wrecked footbridge had become the harbouring fort for all the debris, branches and monstrous tree-trunks which the river swept along its course. The river was still swelling. More accumulation arrived each moment, ramming and pressing the bridge. Under pressure it was cracking and shifting minutely towards a turbulent forty-foot fall.

Gustus had seen it! A feeling of dismay paralysed him, reminding him of his foolish venture. He scraped his cheek on the bank looking back. But how can he go back. He has no strength to go back. His house is nearer than the school. An' Pappy will only strap him for nothin' ... for nothin' ... no shoes, nothin' when the hurricane is gone.

With trembling fingers he tied up the remnants of his shirt. He made a bold step and the wind half-lifted him, ducking him in the muddy flood. He sank to his neck. Floating leaves, sticks, coconut husks, dead ratbats and all manner of feathered creatures and refuse surrounded him. Forest vines under the water entangled him. But he struggled desperately until he clung to the laden bridge, and climbed up among leafless branches.

His legs were bruised and bore deep scratches, but steadily he moved up on the slimy pile. He felt like a man at sea, in the heart of a storm, going up the mast of a ship. He rested his feet on a smooth log that stuck to the water-splashed heap like a black torso. As he strained up for another grip the torso came to life and leaped from under his feet. Swiftly sliding down, he grimly clutched some brambles.

The urgency of getting across became more frightening, and he gritted his teeth and dug his toes into the debris, climbing with maddened determination. But a hard gust of wind slammed the wreck, pinning him like a motionless lizard. For a minute the boy was stuck there, panting, swelling his naked ribs.

He stirred again and reached the top. He was sliding over a breadfruit limb when a flutter startled him. As he looked and saw the clean-head crow and glassy-eyed owl close together, there was a powerful jolt. Gustus flung himself into the air and fell in the expanding water on the other side. When he surfaced, the river had dumped the entire wreckage into the gurgling gully. For once the wind helped. It blew him to land.

Gustus was in a daze when he reached his house. Mud and rotten leaves covered his head and face, and blood caked around a gash on his chin. He bent down, shielding himself behind a tree-stump whose white heart was a needly splinter; murdered by the wind.

He could hardly recognise his yard. The terrorised trees that stood were writhing in turmoil. Their thatched house had collapsed like an open umbrella that was given a heavy blow. He looked the other way and whispered, 'Is still dere! Dat's a miracle . . . Dat's a miracle.'

Dodging the wind, he staggered from tree to tree until he got to his own tormented banana tree. Gustus hugged the tree. 'My nable string!' he cried. 'My nable string! I know you would stan' up to it, I know you would.'

The bones of the tree's stalky leaves were broken, and the wind lifted them and harrassed them. And over Gustus's head the heavy fruit swayed and swayed. The props held the tree, but they were squeaking and slipping. And around the plant the roots stretched and trembled, gradually surfacing under loose earth.

With the rags of his wet shirt flying off his back, Gustus was down busily on his knees, bracing, pushing, tightening the props. One by one he was adjusting them until a heavy rush of wind knocked him to the ground. A prop fell on him, but he scrambled to his feet and looked up at the thirteen-hand bunch of bananas. 'My good tree,' he bawled, 'hol' yo' fruit . . . keep it to yo' heart like a mudder savin' her baby! Dohn let the wicked wind t'row you to the groun' . . . even if it t'row me to the groun'. I will not leave you.'

But several attempts to replace the prop were futile. The force of the wind against his weight was too much for him. He thought of a rope to lash the tree to anything, but it was difficult to make his way into the kitchen, which, separate from the house, was still standing. The invisible hand of the wind tugged, pushed and forcefully restrained him. He got down and crawled on his belly into the earth-floor kitchen. As he showed himself with the rope, the wind tossed him, like washing on the line, against his tree.

The boy was hurt! He looked crucified against the tree. The spike of the wind was slightly withdrawn. He fell, folded on the ground. He lay there unconscious. And the wind had no mercy for him. It shoved him, poked him, and molested his clothes like muddy newspaper against the tree.

As darkness began to move in rapidly, the wind grew more vicious and surged a mighty gust which struck the resisting kitchen. It was heaved to the ground in a rubbled pile. The brave wooden hut had been shielding the banana tree, but in its death-fall missed it by inches. The wind charged again and the soft tree gurgled – the fruit was torn from it and plunged to the ground.

The wind was less fierce when Mr Bass and a searching-party arrived with lanterns. Because the bridge was washed away, the hazardous roundabout journey had badly impeded them.

Talks about safety were mockery to the anxious father. Relentlessly he searched. In the darkness his great voice echoed everywhere, calling for his boy. He was wrenching and ripping through the house wreckage when suddenly he vaguely remembered how the boy had been fussing with the banana tree. Desperate, the man struggled from the ruins, flagging the lantern he carried.

The flickering light above his head showed Mr Bass the forlorn and pitiful banana tree. There it stood, shivering and twitching like a propped-up man with lacerated throat and dismembered head. Half of the damaged fruit rested on Gustus. The father hesitated. But when he saw a feeble wink of the boy's eyelids he flung himself to the ground. His bristly chin rubbed the child's face while his unsteady hand ran all over his body. 'My bwoy!' he murmured. 'Mi hurricane bwoy! The Good Lord save you . . . Why you do this? Why you do this?'

'I did wahn buy mi shoes, Pappy. I . . . I cahn go anywhere 'cause I have no shoes . . . I didn' go to school outing at the factory. I didn' go to Government House. I didn' go to Ol' Fort in town.'

Mr Bass sank into the dirt and stripped himself of his heavy boots. He was about lacing them to the boy's feet when the onlooking men prevented him. He tied the boots together and threw them over his shoulder.

Gustus's broken arm was strapped to his side as they carried him away. Mr Bass stroked his head and asked how he felt. Only then, grief swelled inside him and he wept.

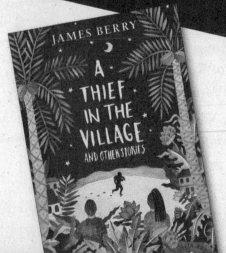

JAMES BERRY

A THIEF IN THE VILLAGE
AND OTHER STORIES

ABOUT THE AUTHOR

JAMES BERRY

1924	Born 28 September in Boston, a rural village in Jamaica, the fourth in a family of six children
1942	When he is eighteen, James goes to work in the USA as a farm labourer during the Second World War
1948	Moves to England where he studies at night school. Works during the day as a telegraphist for the General Post Office while writing stories and poems
1979	His first poetry collection, Fractured Circles, is published
1981	Wins the National Poetry Society's Annual Prize, the first poet of West Indian origin to do so, for Fantasy of an African Boy
1987	A Thief in the Village is published and is the Grand Prix winner of the Smarties Prize

1988	Anancy-Spiderman – *stories about the African folktale character Anancy and his companions Bro Monkey, Bro Dog and Bro Tiger – is published*
1989	*Wins the Signal Poetry Award for* When I Dance *and receives the American Coretta Scott King Honor for* A Thief in the Village
1990	*Made Officer of the Order of the British Empire (OBE) for his poetry*
1991	*Wins the Cholmondeley Award.* The Future-Telling Ladies & Other Stories *is published*
1993	*His short children's novel* Ajeemah and his Son *is awarded the Boston Globe Horn Book award*
1995	*His* Song of a Blue Foot Man *is adapted for stage*
1996	Playing a Dazzler *and* Don't Leave an Elephant to Go and Chase a Bird *are published*
1997	First Palm Trees *is published*
2002	Nest Full of Stars *is published*
2004	*James is judged one of fifty black and Asian writers who have made major contributions to contemporary British literature.* Only One of Me: Selected Poems *is published*
2011	*His last work for adults,* A Story I Am In: Selected Poems, *is published*
2012	*The British Library acquires the archives of his work*

INTERESTING FACTS

As a young child James loved the stories of Anancy the spiderman and folklore of the West Indies. He began writing his own stories when he was still at school.

In his poems, James uses a mixture of standard English and Creole, the language of Jamaica.

During the Second World War, James moved to America to work on a farm, but he found that he did not like it there. He especially disliked the way black people were being treated, so he decided instead to move to the UK in 1948.

James was awarded an honorary doctorate by the Open University and is an Honorary Fellow at Birkbeck College in London.

James was awarded the Smarties Prize for *A Thief in the Village* in 1987.

WHERE DID THE
STORY COME FROM?

*James Berry grew up in Fair Prospect, a small seaside
village in Jamaica surrounded by orange trees, coconut
palms and poinciana trees. He loved reading books as
a child, and especially loved traditional folk tales from
which he drew his inspiration.*

GUESS WHO?

A *He is strong and tough. His pair of little pestle legs and bare feet know every village lane and bush track in the surrounding hills.*

B *I began to blow a tune on my comb and had to stop. The boys were laughing too much. They laughed so much they staggered about. Other children came up and laughed too. It was all silly, laughing at me.*

C *His toothbrush moustache moved about a bit as he said, 'The storm's bad, chil'run. Really bad. But it'll blow off . . .'*

D   *I opened out my brown paper parcel. I showed him my dad's sun helmet. I told him I thought it would make a good fireman's hat.*

E   *. . . was the only village schoolgirl to go 'walking property', and with a gun, though it was her first time. After it, both girls and boys at school never stopped asking her questions about it. They made it look as if she'd been overseas or to the moon or something.*

WORDS GLORIOUS WORDS!

Lots of words *have several different meanings – here are a few you'll find in this Puffin book. Use a* **dictionary** *or look them up* **online** *to find other definitions.*

mouth-organ *also known as a harmonica*

plantain *a fruit similar to a banana, native to tropical countries*

belligerent *to be very aggressive and hostile*

interloper *an uninvited guest*

belfry *a bell tower that is part of a church*

pandemonium *chaos and disorder*

QUIZ

Thinking caps on – Let's see how much you can remember! Answers are at the bottom of the opposite page. *(No peeking!)*

1 *What kind of animal is Misschief?*

a) *A rabbit*

b) *A horse*

c) *A cat*

d) *A dog*

2 *How did Becky get her bicycle?*

a) *She stole it*

b) *She built it herself*

c) *Her mother bought her one*

d) *A fireman gave it to her*

3 What colour is Delroy's mouth-organ?

a) Red

b) Green

c) Blue

d) Orange

4 What is the name of Tukku-Tukku's rival?

a) Stephen

d) Raphael

c) Samson

d) Wildo

5 Where is Jamaica?

a) The Caribbean

b) Africa

c) Asia

d) The South Pacific

ANSWERS: 1) b   2) d   3) a   4) c   5) a

IN THIS YEAR

Margaret Thatcher is re-elected as Prime Minister of the United Kingdom.

The Great Storm of 1987 takes place in October, claiming the lives of *twenty-two people*, and is considered to be the *worst storm* in the UK in nearly three hundred years.

Fire breaks out in *King's Cross* tube station in London, having been *accidentally* started on an escalator.

The Simpsons is seen for the very first time on television!

MAKE AND DO

Make your own *ice-lolly-stick harmonica!*

If Delroy's attempt to make a mouth-organ (aka harmonica) out of a comb inspired you, try making your own musical instrument too. It's easy! Pick your favourite colour and decorate yours to reflect your style.

YOU WILL NEED:

* 2 ice-lolly sticks
* 2 rubber bands
* 2 toothpicks cut to the width of the ice-lolly sticks
* A strip of ordinary paper, the same size as the ice-lolly stick
* Some watercolours

1 Pick a colour for your very own harmonica, then paint the lolly sticks and allow them to dry.

2 Once the ice-lolly sticks are dry, place your piece of paper between them.

3 Carefully wrap a rubber band round and round one end.

4 Place one of the pieces of toothpick on the inside, right next to the rubber band.

5 Repeat instructions 3 and 4 on the other side of the ice-lolly stick.

6 Hold the sticks to your mouth and try blowing through it to make tuneful sounds!

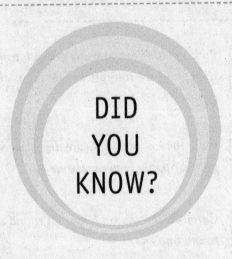

DID
YOU
KNOW?

Reggae music originally comes from Jamaica.

Thanks to the **mongoose** there are now very few snakes living in Jamaica.

Jamaica lies in the **hurricane belt** of the Atlantic Ocean, which is why there are so many **violent storms**, like the ones described in James Berry's stories.

PUFFIN
WRITING
TIP

When James **first started** writing down his poems and stories, he **didn't use a computer**. The best writers **always** carry a **pen and notebook** with them. Next time you go outside, take your pen and paper with you and **jot down** what you **see, hear** and **smell**.

A Puffin Book can take you to amazing places.

WHERE WILL YOU GO?

#PackAPuffin

HOW MANY HAVE YOU READ?

stories that last a lifetime

Animal tales

- ☐ The Trumpet of the Swan
- ☐ Gobbolino
- ☐ Tarka the Otter
- ☐ Watership Down
- ☐ A Dog So Small

War stories

- ☐ Goodnight Mister Tom
- ☐ Back Home
- ☐ Carrie's War

Magical adventures

- ☐ The Neverending Story
- ☐ Mrs Frisby and the Rats of NIMH
- ☐ A Wrinkle in Time

Unusual friends

- ☐ Stig of the Dump
- ☐ Stuart Little
- ☐ The Borrowers
- ☐ Charlotte's Web
- ☐ The Cay

Real life

- ☐ Roll of Thunder, Hear My Cry
- ☐ The Family from One End Street
- ☐ Annie
- ☐ Smith

stories that last a **lifetime**

Ever wanted a friend who could take you to magical realms,
talk to animals or help you survive a shipwreck? Well, you'll find
them all in the **A PUFFIN BOOK** collection.

A PUFFIN BOOK will stay with you **forever**.
Maybe you'll read it again and again, or perhaps years from now
you'll suddenly **remember** the moment it made you **laugh** or
cry or simply see things **differently**. Adventurers **big** and **small**,
rebels out to **change** their world, even a mouse with a **dream**
and a spider who can spell – these are the characters who
make **stories** that last a **lifetime**.

Whether you love animal tales, war stories or want to
know what it was like growing up in a different time and place,
the **A PUFFIN BOOK** collection has a story for you
– you just need to decide where you want to go next . . .